Just as she was about to turn toward her vehicle, which was parked in his driveway, Kayley glanced down.

And that was when she saw it. There was a bright, shiny new penny right in her path.

Without giving it a second thought, Kayley quickly bent down to pick it up. She'd stopped abruptly without giving Luke any warning, making him walk right into her as she stooped over the coin.

The unexpected contact almost caused her to pitch forward, and she would have done just that had Luke not grabbed for her, pulling her to her feet and throwing her off balance. Her body hit his. Air whooshed out of her and she found herself looking right up at him with less than half an inch between them.

Temptation, fast and furious, appeared out of nowhere, taking control while his brain went on temporary hiatus for about ten seconds.

Before he realized what he was doing—and the consequences that would come with it—Luke found himself kissing Kayley.

MATCHMAKING MAMAS: Playing Cupid. Arranging dates. What are mothers for?

P9-DNV-255

Dear Reader,

Every story comes from somewhere. This story has its origin from two different sources. A friend who truly believed that the pennies she found in her path were a form of communication by her late mother—telling that friend that her mother was watching over her—and a short article about a movie star who was revisiting fatherhood for a second time. Trying to be a good dad, he had joined forces with his imaginative young daughter, who was determined to catch a leprechaun. Reading it brought a smile to my face. So much so that I cut the article out and reread it whenever I felt a little down—hey, it happens. I wanted to bring that smile to you as well as that feeling that loved ones who've left us are still with us in a way.

This book was written in December, when the hustle of Christmas was all around us. It's a time of year that's very special to me. It's also a time of year, despite having my family with me, that I really miss my mother a great deal. When I was growing up, she was Christmas to me. She always found a way to put something under the tree even when we were living hand to mouth. People we love never leave us. They're always there, in our hearts and in everything we do.

As always, I thank you for taking the time to read my book and from the bottom of my heart, I wish you someone to love who loves you back.

All the best,

Marie

A Second Chance for the Single Dad

Marie Ferrarella

H **HARLEQUIN**® SPECIAL EDITION®

If you purchased this book without a cover you should be aware that this book is stolen property. It was reported as "unsold and destroyed" to the publisher, and neither the author nor the publisher has received any payment for this "stripped book."

Recycling programs
for this product may
not exist in your area.

ISBN-13: 978-0-373-62357-0

A Second Chance for the Single Dad

Copyright © 2017 by Marie Rydzynski-Ferrarella

All rights reserved. Except for use in any review, the reproduction or utilization of this work in whole or in part in any form by any electronic, mechanical or other means, now known or hereinafter invented, including xerography, photocopying and recording, or in any information storage or retrieval system, is forbidden without the written permission of the publisher, Harlequin Enterprises Limited, 225 Duncan Mill Road, Don Mills, Ontario M3B 3K9, Canada.

This is a work of fiction. Names, characters, places and incidents are either the product of the author's imagination or are used fictitiously, and any resemblance to actual persons, living or dead, business establishments, events or locales is entirely coincidental.

This edition published by arrangement with Harlequin Books S.A.

For questions and comments about the quality of this book, please contact us at CustomerService@Harlequin.com.

® and TM are trademarks of Harlequin Enterprises Limited or its corporate affiliates. Trademarks indicated with ® are registered in the United States Patent and Trademark Office, the Canadian Intellectual Property Office and in other countries.

Printed in U.S.A.

www.Harlequin.com

USA TODAY bestselling and RITA® Award–winning author **Marie Ferrarella** has written more than two hundred and seventy-five books for Harlequin, some under the name Marie Nicole. Her romances are beloved by fans worldwide. Visit her website, marieferrarella.com.

Books by Marie Ferrarella

Harlequin Special Edition

Matchmaking Mamas

Meant to Be Mine
Twice a Hero, Always Her Man
Dr. Forget-Me-Not
Coming Home for Christmas
Her Red-Carpet Romance
Diamond in the Ruff
Dating for Two
Wish Upon a Matchmaker
Ten Years Later...
A Perfectly Imperfect Match
Once Upon a Matchmaker

The Fortunes of Texas: The Secret Fortunes

Fortune's Second Chance Cowboy

Montana Mavericks: The Baby Bonanza

A Maverick and a Half

Montana Mavericks: What Happened at the Wedding?

Do You Take This Maverick?

The Fortunes of Texas: Cowboy Country

Mendoza's Secret Fortune

Visit the Author Profile page
at Harlequin.com for more titles.

To
Dr. Johnson,
Dr. Younger,
Dr. Kang
And all the others who
Worked hard to put me back together
This year
Thank you
I now know what Humpty Dumpty
Felt like

Prologue

One moment the blond-haired, attractive woman with the kind blue eyes wasn't there; the next moment, she was. Her very presence seemed to dominate the real estate office, an office devoted to a business that Maizie Sommers had taken such pride in building up over the years.

The only business that Maizie took even more pride in was the one that she and her two lifelong best friends, Theresa Manetti and Cecilia Parnell, conducted unofficially. A business that yielded no monetary rewards. However, the rewards that it did yield were far richer than any dollar amount.

And it was as if the woman standing before her now sensed that fact despite that they had never really talked about it.

"Maizie," the woman said in a soft voice, "you need

to help Kayley find someone. I don't want her spending the rest of her life alone. It's not right. She has so much love to give and no one to give it to. I'd find her someone myself, but I can't do that now. And she is your goddaughter," Karen Quartermain added pointedly. "Help her, Maizie. Please."

The woman's quietly worded request seemed to fill up every single space within the room.

Gasping, Maizie bolted upright. She wasn't in her office—she was in her bed.

Her bedroom was dark, except for the ray of moonlight intruding like a laser through the window. It was shining on something on the rug. Something small and round.

Blowing out a long breath, Maizie ran her hand along her forehead.

A dream. It was only a dream.

Her brain should have realized that even though every detail had seemed so incredibly vivid and real. Her office had looked just like her office. And her friend had looked just like her friend. Except that Karen had looked the way she had a year ago, before she became ill.

Why in heaven's name was she dreaming about Karen Quartermain, Maizie silently asked herself. She'd never dreamed about Karen, even when she was alive. Why now, two months after her friend had died?

With a sigh, Maizie lay back down. It was still very early. Turning on her side, she faced the window. She inhaled deeply and willed herself to get back to sleep.

Vivid or not, it was just a dream, nothing more. Nothing—

What was that on her rug?

The moonlight made her light gray rug appear pale even as it highlighted something on it.

Whatever it was looked as if it were winking at her.

Maizie sighed again. She was going to drive herself crazy guessing.

She wouldn't have any peace until she found out what was on the rug. Throwing off her covers, Maizie got up and went to see exactly what the moonlight was shining on.

It was a penny.

What was a penny doing on her rug? The only explanation she could think of was that it must have fallen out of her pocket when she had gotten undressed for bed last night. But why had it been in her pocket in the first place? She never kept change in her pocket.

After picking it up, she sat down on the edge of her bed, staring at the coin. She was *certain* she hadn't put it into her pocket. Any pennies she acquired went into a glass jar in her office and she hadn't acquired any in a while.

"Karen?" she finally said uneasily, glancing around her bedroom. "Is this from you? Is this your way of giving me a sign?"

She knew it would have seemed silly to a great many people, thinking that the penny had just mysteriously appeared, a sign from a world that had no physical boundaries. But she and Karen Quartermain went back a long way. Karen had once jokingly said that if she died before Maizie and ever wanted to communicate, she'd drop a penny in her path so that she would know that she was trying to send a message, that Karen wanted something from her.

Karen had said the same thing to her daughter. Then

she'd laughed, saying that was all pennies were good for these days—communication—since it took too many to buy anything.

Maizie closed her fingers around the penny, holding it as tightly as she had once held her friend's hand as Karen was slipping away.

"That *was* you, wasn't it?" Maizie whispered into the darkness. "That was you, asking me to find someone for Kayley."

It was no longer a question. It was, Maizie thought, an assignment. One she felt honor bound to take on.

"Okay, Karen," she said, completely awake now. "I'll see what the girls and I can do."

Chapter One

"If you don't mind my saying so, Dr. Dolan, you look a little lost. Is there anything I can do for you?" Cecilia Parnell asked kindly.

As was her habit since she'd begun her house-cleaning service—long before she had the large staff of excellent workers that she had now—Cilia would come by and personally check in with her clients once a month to make sure everything was more than satisfactory as far as the service went. Ordinarily, her clients had nothing but praise for the women in Cilia's employ.

But this admittedly was not an ordinary situation.

Cilia had taken a special interest in Dr. Lucas Dolan ever since he had abruptly returned from serving his country overseas. A highly respected orthopedic surgeon who was also a reservist, he had selflessly done two tours of duty in the Middle East, seeing to the needs of not only wounded US soldiers but the native population, as well, many of whom had never even been to a doctor.

And then a call had come nine months ago that changed everything.

His wife, Jill, was driving their four-year-old daughter, Lily, home from preschool when she was broadsided by a driver texting to her boyfriend. Jill and Lily were rushed to the hospital. Luke flew home immediately, praying all the way. But Jill died before he could reach her bedside.

Lily had sustained cuts and bruises and was shaken up by the accident, but apart from being very confused and frightened, she was all right.

"Lost?" Luke repeated, glancing at the woman whose services Jill had engaged the week that they had moved into their house as a husband and wife.

Sitting in his living room, Luke struggled not to allow the sadness that had become his constant companion to overwhelm him.

Yes, he was lost, Luke thought. Lost because his high school sweetheart, the woman he had come to rely on for absolutely everything, was gone. Jill had generously freed him up so that he could concentrate on being the best surgeon he could be.

And now she'd been ripped out of his life without warning, leaving him not just to cope with all those details she had been so good at attending to, not just to cope with the emptiness that her absence had created, but also to cope with the prospect of being a single father to a little girl he hardly knew.

Sometimes it was almost too much for him to bear.

Lily was two when his reserve platoon had been

called up and sent overseas. She was four when he came back into her life.

Now she was five, and things were somewhat better between them. But, like a blind man, Luke was still trying to find his way around in a world that was totally unknown to him.

He forced himself to smile at Cilia, knowing that the older woman was only trying to be kind. But as far as her question went, he couldn't open up to her any more than he could open up to his mother-in-law. Barbara Baxter had moved in to help bridge the gap for Lily after her only daughter had died. Barbara was still there, taking care of Lily since he'd gone back to work.

Because Cilia appeared to be waiting for more of a response from him, he grasped at the first thing that came to mind.

"I'm just a little stressed out, I guess," he told her. "I went back to my old orthopedic medical group recently and so far, I've been sharing the services of a physician's assistant with another one of the surgeons. But I can see it's exhausting for her, trying to be accommodating to my patients as well as his. I've been looking into hiring a physician's assistant of my own, but finding the right person has turned out to be more challenging than I thought."

"Really?" Cilia said sympathetically. "Well, I have the occasion to interact with a lot of people in my line of work, not to mention that my two closest friends have their own businesses, as well, and they come in contact with an even larger variety of people than I do. I'll tell them to keep an eye out for a possible candidate for you to interview. I'm sure that between the three of us, we'll have you set up with someone more than suitable for your needs in no time," Cilia promised with a warm, motherly smile.

"I'm looking for a *physician's assistant*," Luke emphasized, wanting to be absolutely clear that she understood what he needed.

Cilia's smile widened. "But of course—I understand completely," she told him. "I'll let you know the moment one of my friends or I find one," she promised. "Always a pleasure talking to you, Doctor."

She nodded at Luke's mother-in-law as she passed the woman on her way out.

Barbara had filled her in on her son-in-law's story, sharing with her that she was worried about Luke. He was like a fish out of water without Jill in his life, she'd told Cilia. It was obvious that Barbara grieved for the loss of her daughter, but Cilia could tell that the woman also grieved for Luke and for Lily. She and Barbara were in agreement that Luke needed a wife and Lily needed a mother, and Barbara was unselfish enough to realize that.

Aware of what she and her two friends did on the side, Barbara had called and spoken to Cilia earlier today, appealing to her as a mother—and a grandmother. Quite blatantly, Barbara had asked Cilia for her help.

It was what had prompted Cilia's visit today, since Barbara had told her that her son-in-law had taken the day off.

Cilia had wanted to feel Luke out for herself. Looking into the handsome thirty-eight-year-old's eyes and exchanging a minimum of words, Cilia had decided that the young doctor was definitely someone she and her friends could help.

Indeed, they *needed* to help the man who had suffered such a terrible loss while he'd been nobly serving his country.

Leaving the doctor's house, Cilia couldn't wait to talk to her friends. She called Maizie and Theresa from her car before she even started it, suggesting they get together that evening to play cards, which had become their euphemism for undertaking the very challenging task of matchmaking.

"I've got a candidate for us!" Cilia declared as she crossed the threshold later that evening, walking into Maizie's living room.

"We're in here," Theresa called out to her from the family room.

The moment Cilia entered the family room, where all their card games took place, Maizie told her, "Cilia, you took the words right out of my mouth."

Slightly puzzled, Cilia looked at her friend. "I was the one who called for a meeting," she reminded Maizie.

"Only because I haven't had a chance to," Maizie answered. "I was busy meeting with our next matchmaking candidate."

Cilia was accustomed to Maizie being the unofficial leader of their group. She always had been. But this one time, she decided to dig in her heels. "I think my candidate needs our attention first."

Maizie wasn't used to arguing, but she stuck to her guns—because this was personal. "Mine's my goddaughter."

One of the reasons they had remained such close friends over the decades, weathering good times and bad, was that none of them pulled rank or disregarded the other two. Because it sounded as if this match Maizie had brought up was so important to her, Cilia inclined her head in agreement.

Sitting down at the card table where they did all their best brainstorming, Cilia said, "All right, it's your house, Maizie. You go first."

As she began to tell Theresa and Cilia about what had inspired her to take on this match, she wondered if her friends were going to think she had gone over the deep end.

She looked from Theresa to Cilia. "You two remember my friend Karen Quartermain, don't you?"

Theresa's response was an animated "Of course."

Cilia looked momentarily saddened as she told Maizie, "Karen was much too young when she died."

Maizie nodded. "Agreed. Karen always said that if she died first and ever needed to get me to do something, she'd find a way to drop a penny in my path so I'd know she was trying to communicate with me."

She gazed at the two women she'd been friends with since the third grade. She was fairly certain that they would understand what she was about to say next, but she wasn't 100 percent convinced. Mentally crossing her fingers, she continued.

"I dreamed about her last night. It was a very vivid, very real dream. She asked me to find someone for her daughter, Kayley. When I woke up, there was a penny on my carpet. I have no idea how it got there, but I *know* it wasn't there when I went to bed."

Cilia studied her closely. "Are you sure about that?"

"Absolutely," Maizie answered with feeling. "Kayley is a wonderful girl. She gave up her job at a medical clinic in San Francisco to come home and nurse her mother through her final stages of bone cancer."

The words *medical clinic* instantly caught Cilia's attention. "What did she do at the medical clinic?" Cilia asked.

"Kayley's a physician's assistant. I can't tell you what a comfort she was to her mother— What?" Maizie asked, seeing the wide smile on Cilia's face.

Cilia suppressed a laugh. "I think that you just came up with the perfect solution for both of us," she told Maizie.

It was Maizie's turn to be confused. "Come again?" she asked uncertainly.

Cilia's face was a wreath of smiles as she happily said, "Trust me, I have the perfect guy for your god-daughter."

Kayley Quartermain glanced at the address on the piece of paper that her godmother, Maizie Sommers, had given her.

After her college graduation, Kayley hadn't seen the woman she called Aunt Maizie for several years. Then Maizie had visited a week before her mother died. Maizie had been upset that she hadn't heard about Karen being sick until the cancer had reached stage four. It was Aunt Maizie who had kept Kayley from going to pieces. She'd also been the one to help her with her mother's funeral arrangements.

Looking back now, Kayley had to admit that she didn't know what she would have done without her godmother's help.

She laughed softly to herself as she pulled into the medical building's parking lot. Aunt Maizie was more like a *fairy* godmother than just a run-of-the-mill god-mother, Kayley thought. Not only had she helped to get her through what had to be the worst point in her life, but just last night, Aunt Maizie had called her to say that she thought she had found a possible position for her. She had a friend who knew a surgeon reestablishing his practice and he needed—wait for it, she mused with a smile—a physician's assistant.

Maybe life was taking a turn for the better after all, Kayley thought, pulling her car into the first space she found.

It was a tight fit, requiring her to pay close attention to both sides of her vehicle as she pulled into the spot. Getting out of the car, she found she had to inch her way out slowly in order to keep from pushing her car door into the other vehicle.

Being extra careful, she eased her door closed and fervently hoped that the owner of the car next to hers would be gone by the time she was finished with her job interview.

She moved away from her door, backed out gingerly, then turned to make her way to the entrance of the two-story medical building.

Which was when she saw it.

There, right in front of her just as she was about to walk to the entrance of the building, was a bright, shiny new penny.

She stared at it for a moment, thinking she was imagining it.

Ever since her mother had died, she'd been on the lookout for pennies, even though she told herself she was being foolish because only a fool would really believe that her late mother would be sending her a sign from heaven.

But there it was, a penny so new that it looked as if it had never been used.

Unable to help herself, Kayley smiled as she stooped down to pick up the coin.

She was also unable to keep herself from wondering, *Does this mean I'm going to get the job, Mom? That you somehow arranged all this for me?*

Even as the question darted across her mind, she knew it was silly to think like this. Logically, she knew that the departed couldn't intervene on the behalf of the people they had left behind.

She was letting her loss get to her.

And yet…

And yet here was a penny, right in her path. And now right in the middle of her hand.

Was it an omen, a sign from her mother that this—and everything else—was going to work out well for her?

She really wanted to believe that.

Kayley caught her lower lip between her teeth and looked at the penny again.

"Nothing wrong in thinking of it as a good-luck piece, right?" she murmured under her breath, tucking the coin into her purse.

Lots of people believed in luck. They had lucky socks they wore whenever they played ball, lucky rabbits' feet tucked away somewhere on their bodies when they took tests.

They believed that luck—and objects representing that luck—simply tipped the scales in their favor.

Nothing wrong with that, Kayley told herself again.

Thinking of the penny in her purse, she squared her shoulders and walked up to the entrance of the medical building.

The electronic doors pulled apart, allowing her to walk in. The entrance, she realized, opened automatically to accommodate people who might have trouble pulling open a heavy door because of conditions that brought them to an orthopedic surgeon in the first place.

Once inside the building, Kayley moved aside, away from the electronic door sensors. She needed to gather herself together in order to focus. She was good at what she did, very good, but she knew that she could still wind up tripping herself up.

You want me to get this job, don't you, Mom? You brought Aunt Maizie back into my life because you knew I was going to need her to get through this. And then, because you were always worried about me, you had her call me about this job opening.

Suddenly wanting to take another look at the penny, Kayley opened her purse and gazed down at it.

You're still looking out for me, aren't you? Kayley silently asked, although, in her heart, she knew the answer to that.

The elevator was just right of the entrance. The elevator doors opened as she walked up to them.

Another good omen? she wondered, trying to convince herself that she was a shoo-in for the job.

The elevator car was empty.

The nerves that usually began to act up each time she had to take on something new—a job interview, an admission exam, anything out of the ordinary—seemed oddly dormant this time.

Kayley smiled to herself. She had a feeling—irrational though it might be—that she wasn't going to be facing this interview by herself. Even so, she did experience a fleeting sensation of butterflies—large ones—preparing to take flight. And quickly.

"It's going to be all right," she promised herself in a low whisper since no one else was in the elevator with her. "Nothing to be afraid of. You're going to be fine. The job's yours."

Just as the doors were about to close again, a tall athletic-looking man with wayward dark blond hair put his hand in.

The doors still closed, then immediately sprang open again, receding back to their corners and allowing him to walk in.

"I'm sorry, did you say something?" he asked, looking straight at her, his head slightly cocked as if he couldn't decide if he'd overheard something he shouldn't have.

"Not a word," Kayley answered brightly.

It was a lie, but she wasn't about to admit to a perfect stranger—and he really *was* perfect—that she was giving herself a pep talk. It would have made him think that he was sharing the elevator with a mildly deranged woman.

That was how rumors got started, she thought, smiling at the man.

He didn't return the smile.

Chapter Two

The Orthopedic Surgeons Medical Building was a square white building that had only two floors. The bottom floor housed an outpatient operating facility as well as an area where MRIs and other diagnostic scans were taken. The front of the second floor was a communal reception area where patients could sign in and then wait to be taken through the double doors to the myriad of rooms that honeycombed the rear of the floor. That was where a variety of orthopedic doctors, each with his or her own specialty, would see them.

When the elevator doors opened on the second floor, the solemn-looking man riding up with her put his hand out again, this time to assure that the car's doors would remain open. Then he stared at her, waiting.

"Oh." Kayley had been lost in thought, but now she came alive, realizing that the strikingly handsome man was holding the doors open for her. "Thank you," she told him quickly, hurrying out of the elevator.

"Don't mention it," the man murmured in a deep voice that seemed to surround her even though there was all this wide-open space around her.

As she tried to orient herself, the first thing Kayley saw was a long dark teak reception desk. There were currently three women seated there, each incredibly perky looking and each busily engaged, typing on computer keyboards.

Kayley waited until one of them was free and then walked up her. It was a petite brunette with lively green eyes.

Giving her a cursory glance, the brunette asked, "Name?"

It had been several years since she'd had to go through the interview process. Kayley felt the tips of her fingers grow icy as she answered, "Kayley Quartermain."

The receptionist skimmed a list she pulled up on her screen. Frowning, she looked up again and asked, "And you're here to see…?"

She'd memorized everything on the piece of paper Aunt Maizie had handed her, but she still looked down at it before answering.

"Dr. Dolan." It felt as if the man's name was sticking to the roof of her mouth.

The receptionist pulled up a new list, this one apparently highlighting that particular doctor's schedule for the day. If anything, the frown on her lips deepened.

"Are you sure you have an appointment?" the woman asked. "I don't see you on Dr. Dolan's list."

"I'm sure," Kayley told her. "I called your office to verify the appointment yesterday afternoon."

The receptionist shrugged and reached toward a shelf where two sets of forms were stacked. "New patient or follow-up?" she asked.

"Oh." It dawned on Kayley that the receptionist was making a mistake. "Neither."

Confusion creased the young woman's high forehead. "Well, then, I'm afraid that you can't—"

"No, you don't understand," Kayley said, cutting her short. "I'm applying for the position of Dr. Dolan's physician's assistant," she explained. "I was told he was looking for one." Then, to back up her claim, she added, "I emailed him my résumé."

The receptionist instantly became friendlier. "Boy, is Rachel going to be happy to see you," she said with enthusiasm.

"Rachel?" Kayley asked uncertainly, not sure what the receptionist was telling her.

"That's Dr. Barrett's physician's assistant," the receptionist explained. "She's helping Dr. Dolan out until he finds his own PA. But she's also working for Dr. Barrett and between the two, she can hardly draw two breaths consecutively." The receptionist lowered her voice. "The poor thing's worn out," she confided.

Kayley nodded sympathetically. "Hopefully, she'll be able to draw a lot of consecutive breathes shortly."

"Yes." The receptionist offered her a quick one-size-fits-all smile and then told her, "Please take a seat in the waiting room. Someone will be with you very shortly."

The "someone" turned out to be the physician's assistant who was currently juggling patients for both Dr. Dolan and Dr. Barrett.

Young and undoubtedly vibrant, Rachel Mathews fairly burst through the double doors that led to the back offices.

After a brief word with the receptionist, the beleaguered physician's assistant made eye contact with her and immediately broke out in a huge relieved smile. Rather than standing and waiting by the door to the back rooms, Rachel swiftly came up to her and put her hand out as she asked hopefully, "You're the one here about the opening for a physician's assistant?"

"Yes, that's—"

Rachel wouldn't even let her finish her sentence. Judging by the young woman's expression, Kayley had the feeling that Rachel was fighting the urge to throw her arms around her.

As it was, Rachel cried, "Thank God! I don't think I could have taken one more week of doing double duty." She shook her hand vigorously. Again, the woman seemed as if she was on the verge of embracing her.

Had she already landed the position? Kayley asked herself. Granted, she was very proud of her medical skills and what she had learned during the last round of courses she had taken to improve upon her degree, but there was no way that this Rachel person could know that. For all she knew, Kayley could have fabricated everything on her résumé.

"Come with me," Rachel told her. "I'll take you to the back and you can tell me about yourself."

"It's all there, in my résumé," Kayley told the back of Rachel's head as the PA led the way through a maze that eventually brought them to a room in the extreme rear.

"It's always good to get the feel of a person," Rachel said. "Looking into a person's eyes tells me more than the words on any résumé."

Taking her into what was clearly an exam room, complete with a monitor that highlighted X-ray films, Rachel gestured for her to take a seat.

"You can sit on either the chair or the exam table, whatever makes you feel the most comfortable." It was obvious by her mechanical tone that she recited those words to anyone she brought into either of the two doctors' exam rooms.

"I'll take the chair," Kayley told her. Sitting on the table would make her feel too vulnerable. As it was, she could feel her fingertips getting cold again.

She handed the woman a copy of the résumé she'd sent the doctor by email and then braced herself for a shower of questions.

The shower didn't come.

Instead, Rachel just began to talk to her. "Dr. Dolan is a really nice man. But the poor man's sad. Very sad. He's going through a rough patch. You shouldn't take that as any kind of reflection on you," Rachel warned.

After having given up a rather lucrative, promising position for a prominent doctor to come back home and nurse her mother, she couldn't afford to be overly picky. Her mother had left her a little bit of money in her will, so there was no need to sell her soul—not until the end of next month, at any rate.

"Is there a reason why he's so sad?" Kayley asked, wondering if there was something that she should know ahead of time. She didn't want to inadvertently make a tactless remark.

"An excellent reason," Rachel told her. "The doctor's

wife was in a car accident and died. His four-year-old daughter was in the car at the time, too, although she's all right now—at least that's what I've heard," Rachel said in a lowered voice. "If you ask me," she continued in an even lower voice, "the doctor blames himself for not being there when it happened."

"There probably wasn't anything he could have done at the time, anyway," Kayley said, thinking of her mother and how hard she'd tried to find a way to get that awful disease to go into remission.

"You're probably right," Rachel agreed. "But word has it that that's not the way he feels, which is all that counts. Anyway—" the physician's assistant shifted her focus and skimmed over the copy of the résumé that Kayley had just handed her "—everything looks in order and I, for one, would love to have you on board," she said with a great deal of enthusiastic sincerity. "But you understand, the doctor has to have the final say."

"Of course," Kayley concurred. She expected nothing less. "To be honest, I thought he'd be the one conducting the interview."

"He's still with his patient, but he'll be here," Rachel promised. "He'll probably ask you a couple of things," the young woman told her. "And, just so that you know, for some reason he turned down the other five applicants."

That didn't sound promising, Kayley thought, her uneasiness growing, although she managed to keep it from Rachel.

"Was there a reason?" she asked, wanting to know what she was up against. If she knew, she might be able to be more in line with what the surgeon was seeking.

But Rachel shook her head. She seemed really disappointed that she couldn't offer anything helpful. "Not that he said. He just shook his head after each of the people he interviewed had left and murmured, 'Not the one.' I thought for sure he clicked with Albert," Rachel told her, and then sighed, "but I was wrong."

"Albert?" she asked.

At least the doctor had no preconceived notions about the person he was looking for to fill the position. If he had, he wouldn't have interviewed a man for it—or if he had set notions, he might have *only* interviewed men for the job.

Rachel nodded. "Albert was the last PA who applied."

This was not shaping up to be particularly encouraging. But then, if this didn't work out, she would be no worse off than she was right now. Besides, she had a ton of her mother's things to go through and if worse came to worse, that would take up a good amount of her time. At least she would stay busy until she was able to find a job.

"Wait right here," Rachel said, about to leave the room. "Dr. Dolan will be with you as soon as he finishes up with his patient," she assured her.

The moment she said the words, Rachel suddenly turned rather pale. "Omigod, I forgot he asked me to bring the last X-rays for Mr. Mulroney." She began to rush out of the room, pausing only to toss a few last words over her shoulder. "I *really* hope you get this job."

The corners of Kayley's mouth curved ever so slightly as she watched the other woman dash out. "Me too, Rachel," she said, knowing that the PA was no longer in earshot. "Me too."

Kayley sat back in her chair and waited.

And waited.

After twenty minutes, she started to grow rather restless. She also started to think that very possibly, she had gotten lost in the shuffle. When she'd come in, she had noticed that there were probably more than two dozen people sitting outside in the waiting room. And although there appeared to be about ten or eleven physicians presently in the building, she could see how she might have just gotten overlooked or even fallen through the cracks.

For the next five minutes, Kayley debated between waiting in the room quietly and going out to see if perhaps her theory was right and she had been forgotten about.

Since she wasn't the type to simply sit on her hands, choice number two won.

Picking up her shoulder bag, Kayley got up and went to the door. She pulled it open with the intention of heading back to the reception desk to find out what was going on.

It all happened so fast her brain almost went numb.

She got as far as taking one step out of the exam room when she walked straight into a tall athletic man in a white lab coat. The scent of musky aftershave immediately filled her senses.

It was the same man she had shared the elevator with, she realized.

The man wasn't a patient. He was a doctor.

Was he *her* doctor? she couldn't help wondering, still trying to get her bearings.

"Hey, slow down," he cautioned, catching hold of

her by her shoulders to steady her. "You create quite a jolt when you walk into a person."

Startled, Kayley tried to back up. "Oh, I'm sorry. I didn't mean to walk into you."

"Well, that's comforting," he commented drolly. Dropping his hands to his sides, he said, "Rachel tells me that you're here to talk about the physician's assistant opening in the staff."

As subtly as she could, she drew in a breath and then answered, "Yes, I am."

Nodding, the doctor gestured toward the chair. "Please, sit down."

Kayley turned and went back into the room, feeling as if she were moving in slow motion. She took a seat as he'd instructed.

Looking up, she saw that the doctor had followed her in and sat down on a stool, the seat she assumed he would have taken when talking with a patient.

He skimmed the résumé that she'd sent via email and that he'd printed up. "I see that all of your experience has been in San Francisco." Setting the paper down, he stared at her. There wasn't even a hint of a smile in his expression. "Why did you leave your last place of employment?"

"I had to," she told him simply.

"Had to?" Luke repeated. The first thing that occurred to him was that she had been asked to leave. "Were you terminated?"

His question jolted her. "Oh no, I wasn't fired. I found out that my mother had cancer and I came back to take care of her."

He gave no indication of what he was thinking when he began to ask, "Did she—"

"Make it?" Kayley supplied, guessing at what the doctor was about to ask. She shook her head. "No, she didn't."

"Oh." That wasn't what he'd been expecting to hear. Over the last nine months, he felt as if everyone had gone on with their lives and he was the only one to have faced such a glaring loss.

The situation felt awkward and for a moment, he had no idea what to say. Finally, he told her, "Well, at least you got to be with her before she passed on." With all his heart, he wished that he had had that same good fortune. There were so many things that had been left unsaid. He would have given anything to have had even just one last day with Jill.

But that simply wasn't in the cards.

"Yes, I did," Kayley replied. What else could she have said? she thought, shifting in her seat.

"So, why are you looking for a position in Bedford?" he asked her bluntly. "Why not just go back to the Bay Area?"

No small talk here. The man's bedside manner really needed work. But then, she wasn't looking for a friend, Kayley reminded herself. She was looking for an employer.

"Well, I'm originally from around here. Staying in Bedford just seemed like the right thing to do. To be honest, I like living in Southern California a lot more than living up in San Francisco. I find that the people are friendlier—and the weather is certainly better," she ended with a smile.

There wasn't a single shred of emotion on his face as he said, "I see."

She could see that her answer had made the man

thoughtful and she couldn't imagine why it would have that kind of an effect on him. She wasn't certain exactly what sort of an answer the doctor wanted. All that she could do was be honest.

"And, when you get right down to it, this *is* home," she added, hoping to move the interview along past what was clearly a sticking point for the doctor for some reason.

Luke nodded. Her response had reminded him that he hadn't been able to get back for Jill's last breath, her last moments.

Realizing that he'd been silent longer than he'd intended, Luke picked up her résumé again and took a breath.

"I'm going to have to check these references out," he informed her.

She'd been braced for a rejection, and she instantly perked up. "Of course." He sounded as if he was about to get up and leave the room. "Is there anything you want to ask me while I'm here?"

"Yes." He looked into her eyes, trying not to get lost in them. "Why a physician's assistant? Why not a doctor?"

"Frankly, there wasn't enough money for me to go to medical school for the length of time it would take me to become a doctor. I was working part-time already and I didn't want to incur a staggering debt that was going to follow me around for the next thirty or so years." She smiled as she added, "Becoming a physician's assistant was as close to becoming a doctor as I could get. And I was always interested in helping people. In healing them."

For a long moment, the doctor merely stared at her.

She couldn't tell what he was thinking and she wondered if she had talked too much.

Mentally, Kayley crossed her fingers.

Chapter Three

There was a knock on the exam room door and the next moment, Rachel stuck her head in.

"I'm *really* sorry to interrupt, Doctor, but your next patient is getting very restless. Mr. Jeffers says he has an appointment with his lawyer right after he sees you and he's worried that he's going to be late. His lawyer charges by the quarter of the hour—whether he's there or not."

Having delivered her message, Rachel flashed an apologetic look in Kayley's direction.

Luke rose from his stool. "Tell Mr. Jeffers I'll be right with him." Turning back to Kayley, he told her, "Thank you for coming in, Ms. Quartermain. I'll be in touch."

Her heart sank a little. Kayley knew what that meant: *Don't hold your breath.*

Still, she wasn't about to be rude. There was protocol to follow. Kayley forced a smile to her lips and went through the motions.

"I'll look forward to your call, Doctor," she told him—or rather his back because Dr. Dolan was already walking out the door and on his way to his impatient patient.

"Well, I tried," she murmured, sticking her hands into her pockets. Her right hand touched the penny she'd found right outside the office. "I guess this wasn't our lucky day after all, Mom," she whispered just before she walked out of the exam room.

Giving in to impulse, Kayley stopped at the supermarket and picked up a consoling pint of rum raisin ice cream. She was tempted to buy two, but she knew that she had absolutely no willpower when she felt this disappointed. That meant that if she bought two pints, she would wind up eating two pints—in one sitting.

Keeping this in mind, Kayley restrained herself, took only the single pint to the checkout counter and then hurried out of the store before she weakened and went back for another one.

With the supermarket doors closing behind her, she stepped off the curb—and saw yet another penny.

"Nice try, Mom," she said with a touch of sarcasm. "But I'm not buying it."

Kayley walked right by the lone penny and was halfway to her car when her desire to think the best of every situation got the better of her. She stopped, turned around and retraced her steps until she was looking down at the penny again.

Picking the coin up, she found that unlike the shiny

one she'd found earlier in front of the medical building, this one was old, worn and sticky. Apparently, some sort of gummy substance had been spilled on it.

Still, now that she'd picked it up, she couldn't just toss it aside. Holding on to the coin, she headed back to where she had parked her car.

"Okay, so sue me. I'm an idiot and I have to believe in something," she muttered as she opened her car. "I have to believe it's going to be all right."

Leaning over in her seat, she put the pint of ice cream on the passenger-side floor. Then she buckled up and drove home planning her evening: consuming a pint of rum raisin ice cream and watching an old movie on one of the classic-movie channels.

Her landline was ringing when she walked in.

Hoping against hope, Kayley dropped her purse on the floor next to the door and, still carrying the bag of ice cream, she quickly made her way over to the phone that was sitting on one of the two side tables bracketing the sofa.

Kayley grabbed the receiver and uttered a breathless "Hello?"

"How did it go?" the cheerful, maternal voice on the other end of the line asked.

Kayley suppressed the sigh that rose to her lips. It was her fairy godmother, calling to check on her. She should have guessed.

"I don't know yet," she told Maizie, temporarily sinking down on the sofa. She tried not to sound as dejected as she felt when she added, "Dr. Dolan said they'd be in touch."

"Yes, but how did it *go*?" Maizie repeated with a

touch of eagerness in her voice. "You must have some sort of impression about the way the interview with Dr. Dolan went."

"As a matter of fact, yes, I do," Kayley answered. "It went fast."

There was a pause on Maizie's end. "I'm not sure I understand," she said.

"The doctor squeezed my interview between seeing two patients. That didn't exactly give him much time to talk to me," Kayley explained. Then, because Maizie had gone out of her way to arrange this interview for her, Kayley decided that it was only right to give her godmother a few more details. "He came in, looked over the copy of my résumé that he'd printed out and asked a couple of questions."

"What kind of questions?" Maizie asked.

She told her godmother the first thing that she remembered. "Dr. Dolan wanted to know why I left San Francisco."

It was obvious by the tone of Maizie's response that the woman thought this was a good thing. There was almost excitement in the older woman's voice as she asked, "And did you tell him that it was to nurse your poor sick mother?"

"Yes, I did, Aunt Maizie," Kayley replied dutifully, smiling at the question.

There was a time when she would have resented being treated like a child, but now that her mother was gone, she had to admit she rather liked it. It took her back to when she was younger and was still someone's little girl. Something that she was never going to be again, she thought sadly.

"And what did he say?"

"Something strange, actually," Kayley answered. "I'm paraphrasing but he said that at least I was lucky enough to be able to be there to share some time with my mother before she died."

"That's because he was serving overseas when his wife was killed," Maizie told her.

Kayley was surprised that Maizie knew that. But then again, Maizie always seemed to know everything.

"The physician's assistant he's sharing with another doctor told me something about that," Kayley admitted.

Maizie's tone brightened a little as she asked, "And then what did he say?"

"He didn't," Kayley told her. "He became very quiet and just stared at my résumé. Then the physician's assistant stuck her head in to tell him that his next patient was becoming restless. That's when Dr. Dolan thanked me for coming in and told me that he would be in touch." Kayley sighed deeply. She was feeling rather dejected. This was the first interview she'd landed since her mother had died and it hadn't gone very well. "Doesn't sound very hopeful, does it, Aunt Maizie?" she asked.

"Oh, on the contrary, dear. It sounds very hopeful," Maizie assured her. "Just remember, not everyone jumps into things the way you and I do," she told her goddaughter. "Some people are quite slow and deliberate. They need to think things over before they make a decision."

Kayley really wanted to believe that, but she didn't quite see it that way. "The other physician's assistant told me that Dr. Dolan had already interviewed five other candidates for the position and he'd turned each one of them down."

"Did she happen to tell you why?" Maizie asked.

Kayley sighed again, feeling more and more certain that she was never going to hear from the doctor again—or if she did, it was going to be because he was turning her down and he didn't like leaving any loose ends.

"No, she hadn't a clue."

As was her custom—because she had always been such an optimist—Maizie took the information in stride. "Well, you'll get the job, dear. He rejected the first five applicants. Six is your lucky number."

Kayley couldn't help but laugh at Maizie's unorthodox reasoning. "Since when?"

"Why, since right now, of course, dear. I'm sure of it. I can feel it in my bones."

"Well, if your bones feel it, then it's bound to happen," Kayley said, humoring the woman although she was definitely *not* optimistic about the outcome. Still, she loved Maizie for trying to bolster her self-confidence this way.

"Listen, Kayley, I have to show a house to a client in half an hour, but I'm free afterward. Why don't you come over for dinner, say at about six thirty? I could use the company."

Kayley knew that her godmother was constantly on the go. She had a busy social life as well as a family consisting of her daughter, her son-in-law and a number of grandchildren she was quite proud of. Aunt Maizie didn't need company. If anything, she needed an occasional moment of solitude. She was proposing the get-together for her sake.

"Thank you, Aunt Maizie, but I'm fine, really," Kayley told her, begging off. "I've got some correspondence to catch up on and there's a pint of ice cream that's been calling my name since I walked in the door."

Maizie wasn't one to force her will on someone else, even when she meant well. "Well, if you're sure," she said, her voice trailing off.

"I'm sure," Kayley assured her. Then, for good measure, because she could almost hear the hesitance in her godmother's voice, she added what she hoped was an emphatic "Really."

She heard the small resigned sigh that escaped from her godmother before Aunt Maizie said, "Call me the minute you get the job."

Thanks for the positive pep talk, but I'm pretty sure I'm not getting the job, Aunt Maizie.

Out loud, Kayley cheerfully promised her, "I will. Now, I've got to go, Aunt Maizie. The ice cream's melting and it really tastes much better if I use a spoon to eat it, not a straw."

"I'll let you go, then," Maizie said. "I've got that house to show. Think positive, Kayley. Good things happen when you're positive," she advised just before she hung up.

"I am thinking positive," Kayley said to the receiver as she replaced it in the cradle. "I'm positive he's not going to call."

Turning away from the phone, Kayley grabbed the bag with the ice cream in it and hurried into the kitchen with it. She could tell that the ice cream was already getting soft.

After taking a spoon out of the drawer, she crossed

to the kitchen table and removed the pint out of the bag. She'd bypassed using the ice-cream scoop and a bowl. There was no reason to get either dirty. She intended to eat the whole thing in one sitting anyway.

"C'mon, rum raisin, you and I are going to make beautiful music together. Console me," she said to the container as she took the lid off and dug her spoon in the cream-colored semisoft surface.

Kayley closed her eyes, savoring the first bite as she slid it between her lips.

Although it tasted delicious as always, it didn't assuage the gaping disappointment she felt burrowing deep into her chest.

She needed a job.

Maybe not this very minute, but soon.

Very soon.

Some people would have eagerly jumped at having so much free time stretching before them, using it to catch up on their reading, watch movies they hadn't gotten around to seeing and in general just enjoy themselves. But she had never been any good at kicking back and doing nothing. The way she saw it, free time didn't mean anything if that was all there was. It was precious only if it was very limited and doled out a tiny bit at a time.

She took another mouthful of ice cream, hoping it would console her. But it didn't.

"Wonderful," she murmured, licking the spoon clean before sinking it into the container again. "Thirty-two years old and I'm sitting in the middle of my kitchen swallowing empty calories, getting fat and spouting philosophy to a pint of rum raisin ice cream," she said critically, shaking her head. "I really hope this isn't a sign of things to come."

Just then the phone rang again. Turning her head toward the sound, she debated letting the answering machine pick up the caller. She just *knew* it was her godmother calling her back with another suggestion. She really wasn't in the mood for another pep talk.

It was the kind of thing that Maizie did. Her godmother wouldn't rest until she got Kayley to either agree to come over or invite Maizie to come to her mother's house.

Her house now, Kayley corrected. Lord, it was hard to think of it that way.

The phone continued to ring.

Kayley pressed her lips together, frustrated. But ignoring the phone and letting the machine pick up was rude and she knew it. And the last person she wanted to be rude to was her godmother since Aunt Maizie had been so good to her. Most kids lost contact with their godmothers by the time they were five or six but Maizie had always been there for her, one way or another. Being rude was no way to pay Maizie back and the woman knew she was home right now.

With a sigh, Kayley momentarily abandoned the dwindling pint of ice cream, leaving it on the kitchen table as she hurried over to the phone.

"Really, I'm fine, Aunt Maizie," she told her godmother the moment she picked up the receiver. "You don't need to keep calling to check up on me."

There was a long pause on the other end of the line, and then she heard a distant-sounding male voice say, "I'm not Aunt Maizie, but I'm glad you're fine."

Dr. Dolan? It couldn't be.

And yet...

Her fingers had gone slack and the receiver almost slipped out of her hand. Getting a better grip on it, Kayley fumbled with an apology. "I'm sorry. I thought you were someone else—"

There was just the slightest hint of a laugh. Or maybe it qualified as only a dismissive chuckle.

"Obviously," the deep voice said.

Her heart was fluttering like a hummingbird.

"Who is this?" she asked uncertainly, although a part of her thought she already knew who it was—but that was probably just wishful thinking on her part.

Nobody called back this fast—unless it was to put her out of her misery by delivering the bad news quickly and cleanly.

Was he calling to do that?

"I'm sorry—let's start over," the man on the other end of the line said. "This is Dr. Dolan. I'm calling to speak to a Ms. Kayley Quartermain. Is this a number where I can reach her? I've already tried the cell phone number on her résumé, but I can't get through to leave a message on her voice mail."

Kayley closed her eyes.

Idiot!

She had to remember to recharge her phone. The battery kept draining and this had to be the third time this week that this had happened, she thought, flustered that she'd committed such a birdbrained oversight.

"Oh, Dr. Dolan, I'm so sorry. This *is* Kayley Quartermain. My cell phone's old and it has trouble holding a charge for more than a couple of hours. It probably died, which is why you couldn't get through."

To her relief, the surgeon took the information in stride. "If that's the case, you might want to look into getting a new cell phone."

"I will," she quickly agreed. "But I've been kind of busy with other things." When he didn't say anything to that, she asked, "Um, is there anything I can help you with?"

He'd probably thought of another question he wanted to ask her. There was no reason for her to get her hopes up. If they were up, they only had that much farther to fall.

Even so, she caught herself crossing her fingers as she waited for the doctor to say something.

"As a matter of fact, there is. How soon can you come in?"

"For another interview?" she asked, not knowing what to make of this.

"You're not being vetted to run for president, Ms. Quartermain," he informed her. "I don't need to conduct another interview. I made a call and talked to the last doctor you worked with. He told me he was very pleased with your work and he wanted to know if there was any way you'd consider coming back." And then he caught her completely by surprise by asking, "Is there?"

"No," Kayley answered, trying to be diplomatic. "I enjoyed my time there and Dr. Andrews was great to work with, but as I told you, Bedford is home and right now I need to feel like I'm home." She paused for a moment. "Is there anything else?"

"Yes, as a matter of fact, there is. You still haven't answered my first question," he told her. "How soon can you come in? And I mean to work."

The hummingbirds began to crash into one another in her chest. "Is now too soon?"

"We're closed now," he said.

"Tomorrow, then." She saw no point in attempting to hide her eagerness.

"Tomorrow," he agreed. "Come in at eight. We'll go over the rules and there's paperwork to fill out." And with that, he hung up.

"Yay!" With a laugh, Kayley threw out what was now incredibly soupy rum raisin, then went to call Maizie with the good news.

Chapter Four

Since returning to the Orthopedic Medical Group, Luke had taken to being the first one in each morning.

Although no specific arrangements had been made regarding this practice, he became the one who usually unlocked the office doors. It wasn't so much that he wanted to get a jump start on the day as he was there to avoid being at home with Lily.

Not that he didn't love his daughter. He loved her a great deal. But he had no idea how to talk to her or how to relate to someone who came up to his belt buckle and with whom he had nothing in common except for the blood that ran through their veins.

He used work as his excuse for getting away. Work was also his excuse for not dealing with the terrible hollow emptiness he felt because Jill was no longer there to act as his go-between.

In addition, being the first in and opening up the office at that time guaranteed Luke at least twenty, possibly thirty, minutes alone. Because his field of expertise ran in a different direction, when he came in, he couldn't get the coffee machine up and running to provide that vital first cup of coffee in the morning. But there was a coffee shop half a block from the medical building and he stopped there first for his daily strong shot of caffeine.

After walking in through the electronic doors, he took the elevator up the single floor and got out. He wasn't prepared to find anyone standing by the locked double doors, waiting.

But there she was, bright eyed and smiling, the woman he had hired the day before. The woman he wasn't 100 percent certain he *should* have hired the day before. But he'd been without a physician's assistant of his own since he'd rejoined the medical group, and while he had a tendency to be oblivious to certain kinds of day-to-day details, even *he* noticed that Rachel, the physician's assistant he was presently sharing with one of his colleagues, looked a little worn around the edges.

As a rule, Luke valued punctuality, but turning up at this hour went far beyond that.

He nodded at his new PA in acknowledgment. "You're here early," he commented as he took out his keys and unlocked the main office doors. "I thought we agreed that you'd be here at eight."

Holding the doors open, he waited for her to walk in first.

"We did," Kayley replied, entering the office. The large reception area was almost eerily quiet. "But I didn't want to take a chance on the morning traffic being heavy and making me late for my first day."

Well, he supposed that was admirable. "What time did you get here?" he asked.

She thought of saying that she wasn't sure, but that would be lying. So she told him the truth, even though it would probably make her seem neurotic in his eyes. "Seven."

Luke glanced at his watch, although he more or less knew what time it was. Seven thirty. So much for his half hour of solitude, he thought, switching the lights on for the entire floor.

"You're going to have to wait for the office manager to get in," he told her. "She's the one who knows which papers you need to fill out."

"That's fine—I understand," she said cheerfully. "I can wait. Is there anything you'd like me to do while I'm waiting?"

Luke hadn't a clue what she was implying, but his mind had a propensity to suggest the worst-case scenario. "Like what?"

She thought of her old office. First thing in the morning, life had been clustered around the coffee machine.

"If you have a coffee machine, I can get the coffee going, if you'd like," she offered.

Luke looked down at the container he had gotten at the coffee shop. "I brought my own," he told her. "But I usually drink more than one cup. And I'm sure everyone else would appreciate starting their day with some hot coffee."

She smiled at him in response. Despite his natural inclination to keep barriers between himself and anyone he interacted with, Luke couldn't help noticing that she had the same kind of smile his daughter had. It was the kind that seemed to light up everything around her.

"Sounds good," Kayley said. "Point me to the coffeemaker."

He paused right outside his own office, which was still closed. "Go straight down that hallway, then turn right at the first opening. The coffeemaker is in the break room. By the time you finish with it, Delia should be in."

She was unfamiliar with the name, since she had met with only him and Rachel, the physician's assistant who had looked so relieved that she was interviewing for the job. "Is that the office manager?"

Luke nodded. "Delia Chin," he said, mentioning the woman's last name as an afterthought.

About to follow the directions he'd just given her to the break room, Kayley abruptly stopped for a second. "Dr. Dolan?"

Luke looked at her over his shoulder. "Yes?"

"Thank you."

There was that smile again, he observed. The next moment, his brow furrowed. "For telling you where the coffee machine is?"

"For hiring me. You won't regret it," she told him, and then hurried off to the break room to get the coffee started before everyone else began arriving.

Luke inserted his key into the lock and opened the door to his private office. "We'll see, Ms. Quartermain," he murmured under his breath. "We'll see."

Kayley could well understand why Rachel had looked so frazzled when they'd met, juggling a full schedule for not just one but two doctors. Handling the peripheral details for Dr. Dolan's patients was challenging enough. It had been only eight hours and Kayley already felt as if she had run two 5K marathons.

She was sitting in the exam room vacated by the doctor's last patient, reviewing what had been entered on the computer, when she felt that someone was standing in the doorway, observing her.

Looking up, Kayley expected to see the doctor with some sort of end-of-day instructions. Instead, it was Rachel.

"So how was your first day?" the other woman asked. It was obvious to Kayley that Rachel was checking in on "the new girl" before she went home.

Kayley paused briefly, wanting to choose exactly the right word. She didn't want to seem ungrateful or to say something that could be misconstrued as a complaint. "It was educational," she finally answered.

Rachel laughed. "Well, I've certainly never heard it referred to as that before. Is Dr. Dolan too much for you?" she asked knowingly. Glancing over her shoulder to make sure she wasn't being overheard, the physician's assistant confided in a lowered voice, "He can be a bit demanding at times."

"Oh no, no. He wasn't too much at all. It just takes some getting used to, that's all. The terminology," she explained. "The last doctor I worked for was a primary physician. Dr. Andrews started his practice long before they had computers in the office. He was a lovely man—kind of like in the mold of an old-fashioned country doctor. If his patients had anything complicated, he usually wound up referring them to other physicians. And he was very laid-back in his approach to his patients. He spent as long as he needed to talking to them—and even more important, listening to them," she added, "so he could get to the bottom of what was bothering them and why they had come to see him."

Kayley smiled fondly, remembering. "He was really challenged having to input everything that transpired during an exam into the computer, so I usually wound up being in the room with him, doing his typing for him. Otherwise, I think he would have seen only one patient an hour."

Rachel nodded sympathetically. "Sounds like you miss him."

"In a way," Kayley admitted, turning back to the computer. "Don't get me wrong, I do enjoy working here. It's just very different. Everything here moves so breathtakingly fast."

"Here one day and you already have a list of suggestions?"

Startled, Kayley froze for a moment, then swiveled the stool she was sitting on around to see that Dr. Dolan was standing behind her.

"Not a list of suggestions, just observations," she told him quickly. She noticed that Rachel had vacated the area, ducking out when Dr. Dolan had appeared. She wished the woman would have given her a warning.

"I see a lot of patients because I want to help a lot of patients. I see no need to linger and talk to them about their hobbies and what baseball team they're rooting for. That kind of thing is just taking time away from another patient I could be helping."

"I realize that, Doctor," she replied. She debated just letting it go at that, but at heart, that wasn't the kind of person she was. She wanted him to understand why she believed in what she'd said. "But taking a couple of minutes just to *talk* to a patient, to set his or her mind at ease, makes them feel that they're something more than just a case file to you."

Luke could feel his temper starting to rise, something that had begun to happen only since he'd lost Jill. It took him a second to get it under control before he spoke.

"Not that I need to justify myself to my new physician's assistant *on her first day of work*," he emphasized, "but I graduated first in my class at Johns Hopkins. I worked hard for that. People come to me not because they want good conversation, but because they want me to put them together when they feel like they're never going to feel whole again. Some other doctor might make them feel all warm and toasty, but I'm the one who's going to put them together, or keep working at it until I'm satisfied that I've done the very best that can be done. *My* very best. If you have a problem with that, then maybe you'd feel better working for someone else."

She surprised him with the enthusiasm in her voice as she answered, "No, I wouldn't." And then she further surprised him with her offer. "I'll take care of the feel-good stuff, and you take care of making them feel whole," Kayley concluded.

Maybe she didn't realize that she had come across as being critical of him. He did a swift review of the day in his mind. She had needed next to no cues from him.

"Well, you did keep things flowing smoothly," he allowed reluctantly, "so we'll give it another day." There was, however, a warning note in his voice.

Kayley heard it and pretended not to. Instead, she smiled as if they were both in agreement. "Thank you, Doctor. I'll see you tomorrow."

"Tomorrow," he repeated, making it sound as if it represented her last chance to get things right.

When Luke stepped off the elevator the following morning, he was only moderately surprised to find Kayley waiting by the office door. Maybe she was afraid that her comment at the end of the day had put her in danger of being fired and she was trying to make up for it.

To support that theory, she had a coffee container in one hand and a large pink box that smelled of something warm and tempting in the other.

"Still attempting to outrun possible traffic?" he asked.

Instead of saying yes or no, she told him, "I hate being late."

He unlocked the main door. "It's an admirable quality, but don't you spend a lot of time waiting around for other people to show up this way?"

She nodded. "But that's still better than being late."

Having unlocked the double doors, he opened one and stepped back to let her enter first.

"Have it your way." And then he nodded at the box Kayley was holding. "What is that, by the way?"

"I brought doughnuts for the office," she told him, heading for the break room.

That seemed a little excessive to him. "How many other people did you offend yesterday?"

His question caught her completely off guard. "Nobody."

"Except for me," Luke pointed out.

She hadn't thought he was really offended. Clearly she'd been mistaken. She quickly rallied. "That was purely unintentional, Doctor—do you like doughnuts?" she asked hopefully.

"No, I don't," he answered sternly. Seeing the disappointment on her face, he relented. "But my daughter does."

"What kind?" Kayley asked. She had picked up a wide variety at the bakery.

Luke shook his head. "I have no idea."

"Then how do you know she likes doughnuts?" Kayley asked innocently.

"My mother-in-law told me." His eyes all but bored into hers. "Any other questions?"

"No, but maybe you should ask your mother-in-law what kind of doughnuts your daughter likes so you could surprise her with them. If you still keep in touch with your mother-in-law," she added, thinking that perhaps, since his wife had died, the man had severed his ties with the older woman.

"Hard not to," he commented as he began to walk away. He had a full day to prepare for and he couldn't do it standing here and talking about doughnuts with Pollyanna. "She lives in my house."

"Oh," was all Kayley said as she went to the break room.

He'd give her one more day, Luke promised himself. And if she continued meddling in his life and his approach to his patients, as well as offering her fortune-cookie pieces of advice, then he'd just have to tell her that her services were no longer needed.

* * *

"I hear you finally have your own physician's assistant," Barbara Baxter said to her son-in-law late that evening, when he finally walked in the door.

He was surprised to find her waiting up for him. He wondered if something was wrong. In addition, her comment caught him entirely off guard. He hadn't mentioned anything about the change at work.

Dropping his briefcase near the front door, Luke asked the stately, attractive older woman, "Where did you hear that?"

"From your new physician's assistant. Kayley called here today," she told him. "She sounds like a lovely young woman."

He was still dealing with the first piece of information. "She called here?" he asked incredulously. "Why on earth would she call?"

"She wanted to know what kind of doughnuts Lily likes," Barbara told her son-in-law. "She said something about sending some home with you tomorrow night. If you ask me, that young woman sounds exceptionally thoughtful. For your sake, I hope that she is as competent as she is thoughtful."

"What she is, Barbara, is very meddlesome. She's been with the medical staff two whole days and she seems to think she can just barge into things."

"Like what kind of things?" Barbara asked, interested.

He answered before he could stop himself. He wasn't usually the type to grouse. "Like telling me how to be a better doctor."

"Can't improve on perfection," Barbara said with a smile.

"I'm not perfect," Luke protested. Did he come off as thinking he was? Nothing could have been further from the truth. "I never said I was."

"No, you didn't," Barbara agreed amicably. "So why didn't you listen to what she had to say?"

"Because *her* idea of being a better doctor is to sit around and just *talk* with the patient. People come to me to be their doctor, not their best friend." Why did he need to defend himself like this? His mother-in-law had been married to a surgeon. Her late husband had actually been his mentor. Barbara of all people should understand how he felt. "I'm sure that they all have enough friends."

"Possibly," Barbara concurred. "But not friends who understand what they're going through, what's wrong with them. That's something that's just unique to you, Lucas. Maybe they just want you to tell them that it's going to be all right."

He sighed, shaking his head. "You're beginning to sound like Kayley," he complained.

But his mother-in-law didn't take it as a complaint. She took it as a confirmation of the other woman's character.

Her brown eyes crinkled as she smiled at him. "And by that you mean that you find her to be intuitive and intelligent?"

He would have laughed, but he felt tired and worn out and whenever he felt like that, the first casualty was his sense of humor.

"You know, Barbara," he told her, beginning to beg off, "it's been a very long day. I think I'll just turn in."

"Don't you want any dinner?" she asked. "Lily insisted I keep it warm for you."

He was certain that it was Barbara, not Lily, who'd thought about maintaining the temperature of his dinner. Luke waved away the notion of eating anything at this late hour. All he wanted was to crawl into his bed and go to sleep.

"They had pizza at the office."

Barbara shook her head, a disapproving expression on her face. "You know, for a doctor you really eat very poorly."

"I had cheese, tomatoes and some dough with a smattering of meat," he said, breaking down what had composed his pizza. "That's four basic food groups. That's better than most."

Barbara looked at him sadly. Luke began to walk away. "You know, I don't remember you being this difficult when I first met you," she called after him.

"A lot of things were different back then," he replied. "For one thing, Jill was still alive."

Barbara bit her tongue.

There were a great many things that she wanted to say to Luke, but she had no idea where or how to start—or how to make him open his eyes. It hurt her to see him like this.

All she could do was hope for a miracle—and hope that it would come before Lucas lost even more time with Lily.

Chapter Five

Exiting the elevator the next day, Luke was rather surprised not to find Kayley waiting by the double doors the way she had been the first two days. He was also relieved, or so he told himself even though it did seem a little strange not to see her there.

His relief, however, was short-lived because as he put his key into the lock for the double doors, he heard the elevator, which was directly on his right, opening its doors.

He didn't have to look to know the lone person getting off was Kayley. The light scent of her perfume—was that lavender?—preceded her.

"Morning, Dr. Dolan," she sang out cheerfully.

"Good morning," he responded in a monotone voice. The door unlocked, and he pushed it open for her. "You know, you don't have to keep coming in early like this. You're not getting paid for this time."

"I know," she replied in what he deemed an annoyingly chipper voice. "I don't mind having a little extra time to set everything up. This way I don't feel as if it's taking time away from the duties that I am being paid for."

Luke stared at her, confused. "'Set up'?" he repeated.

"You know, in the break room." When he continued to look at her blankly, she explained further. "Making coffee."

"Look, I admit that you make really good coffee," he told her—and she did. Somehow, instinctively, she seemed to make it just the way he liked it, dark and rich. The receptionists who took turns making the coffee wound up producing something that tasted as if a brown crayon had been dipped in hot water.

"Thank you!" she cried before he could go on.

The enthusiastic words of gratitude were accompanied by what he had come to regard as that killer smile of hers. Not fully immune to it, Luke made a point of gazing above her head when he addressed her so that it wouldn't cause his attention to deviate.

"But it's not your *job* to make coffee," Luke continued. "That's for one of the administrative assistants to do when they get here. I'm told they take turns." And although none of them seemed to have Kayley's touch, that was beside the point.

"Oh, I really don't mind," she told him. "I like doing it. When I was a little girl, I used to get up early to make my mother coffee. In a way, since she's gone now, making coffee here kind of connects me to her."

At a loss, Luke gave up trying to argue with his PA. Instead, he merely shrugged. "Well, I wouldn't want to deprive you of that. But just remember, you don't have to do this and the moment you get tired of making coffee first thing in the morning, I want you to stop. Nowhere in your job description does it say 'Has to make first pot of coffee in the morning.'"

Her eyes seemed to almost be shining as she said, "I know." About to go, she stopped at the last minute. "Oh. I almost forgot."

Kayley dug into the tan shopping bag she had brought in with her. There was a logo from French's Bakery stenciled on the side of the bag. She took out a small box—there was apparently a much larger box directly beneath it—and handed it to Luke.

He took it warily, the way someone would accept possession of a bomb. There was suspicion in his eyes. "What's this?"

"Sprinkled doughnuts for Lily. Two. I would have gotten her more, but I didn't want her bouncing off the walls for you. And there's also one in there for your mother-in-law. Jelly, not sprinkled," she clarified. There was that smile again. Didn't anything make this woman come down off her cloud? Luke silently demanded. "I got Mrs. Baxter to admit she had a weakness for them."

No doubt about it, he was starting to feel very overwhelmed by this five-foot-four whirling dervish. He didn't think she even came up for air.

"Did someone appoint you goodwill ambassador to the rest of the country somewhere along the line?" he asked, asking the sarcastic question in a less-than-cheerful tone.

"No—but I'm open to the position should there be a need for one," Kayley told him.

And with that, she took her shopping bag filled

with the remaining box of doughnuts and headed for the break room, leaving him staring after her back.

Apparently, sarcasm had no effect on her, Luke concluded. He was at a loss as to what to make of the woman.

In his experience, gifts, even doughnuts, came with strings. There was always some kind of give-and-take involved, or an angle, some piper to pay, a price down the line to be leery of.

But for the life of him, he couldn't discern what that could be in this case. The woman already had the job he assumed she wanted and it wasn't as if the position was a rung on a corporate ladder that she could climb in order to get to more advanced positions.

His eyes narrowed as he tried to get a handle on what she was thinking, what ultimately made his new PA tick. Since he didn't believe in beating around the bush, Luke decided to ask her outright.

He followed her to her cubbyhole of an office. "What's your angle, Kayley Quartermain?" he asked gruffly. "Just what are you after?"

He needed to review some CAT scans before his first patient of the day came in. That was what his early mornings were for, reviewing files, not trying to figure out what was going on in his PA's mind. But he felt he'd have no peace until he at least tried to figure out exactly what she was up to—although he was beginning to think that just might be a lost cause.

She set the box with the doughnuts down on her side table. "I'm not after anything, Doctor," she told him guilelessly. "Do you have all the scans that you need for this morning?" she asked, deftly turning his attention back to his patients.

"Yes," he snapped, then spun on his heel and walked out of her office. He was right—getting down to the bottom of things with her was a lost cause.

Luke had seen seven patients in a row and his morning was going fairly well and without incident—until the last patient he had scheduled before noon arrived.

Ralph Jordan was eleven and he came in with his mother, Janis. It was obvious that he wanted to hold on to his mom's hand, but because he was eleven, like most boys that age, he felt he was too old to do that. So he fidgeted.

From the moment he walked into the exam room, favoring his left leg, it was clear that it was causing him a great deal of pain even though he was attempting to tough it out.

Using a minimum of words, something he had gotten very good at overseas, Luke got down to the heart of the problem. Ralph was a die-hard soccer player, and in his ardor to be the best, he had wound up tearing a ligament in his left leg.

Rather than saying anything to the boy, Luke told Ralph's mother, "I'm going to need an MRI to see the exact nature of the problem."

Other than introducing herself to both the boy and his mother, Kayley had remained quiet during the exam. But now she looked at the boy's face. It was clear that Ralph was more than a little frightened of what lay ahead of him.

"What's that mean?" Ralph asked. When he didn't receive an immediate answer from the doctor, he pressed, "What's an MRI?"

"Just something the doctor has to do," his mother

told him dismissively. The woman appeared to be close to the end of her rope. Not for the first time, Mrs. Jordan glanced at her watch. "Is this going to take long?" she asked nervously.

"It should take about half an hour," Luke told her, giving her a rough estimate. "Fortunately, you don't need to take your son to another building. We have an MRI machine on the first floor." He turned toward Kayley. "Call down to see if the technician is available now to do a scan of the patient's left leg."

"Yes, Doctor."

Kayley checked quickly, and as it turned out, the tech was free. She conveyed the information to both the doctor and the boy's mother.

Luke looked as if he expected nothing less. Mrs. Jordan, however, seemed about to come out of her skin.

Running her tongue along her upper lip, she looked anxiously at the doctor. "I know this is highly irregular, but I have a four-year-old to pick up from preschool. The school's not that far from here," she added hastily, probably hoping that fact would tip the scale in her favor. "Can you do this MRI scan if I leave my son with you? I promise I'll be back within the hour," she said, her eyes all but begging the doctor.

"You can't leave me here, Mom!" Ralph almost shrieked. Visibly scared, the eleven-year-old also sounded as if he was about to have a meltdown at any second.

"Ralph, don't make a scene," Mrs. Jordan ordered. "It'll be all right. Won't it, Doctor?" Again, Ralph's mother silently pleaded with the doctor, this time for some words of encouragement for her son.

Kayley could see that Dr. Dolan didn't have anything like that to give her. It just wasn't his way. She immediately intervened by volunteering. "I can go with him to get the scan, Doctor." Then, turning to the boy, she promised, "It'll be a piece of cake, Ralph."

Kayley could see out of the corner of her eye that her boss was less than thrilled with the way this was all going. But to her, the important one in the room was the boy. She needed to keep him calm.

Ralph's mother looked relieved to be able to have someone take charge of her son while she went to pick up her younger child.

"Thank you, Doctor. Kayley." Janis Jordan expressed her thanks on the run as she hurried out of the room. She was gone before her words registered.

With a garbled cry of protest, the terrified boy grabbed on to Kayley and held on as if letting go meant being forever lost.

Kayley's heart went out to him. There must have been a better way for his mother to have handled this. But then, Kayley told herself, she'd never had two children demanding her time, so she shouldn't be judgmental.

"I'll take him down to radiology now, Doctor," she told Luke.

Ralph tugged on her arm. "What's radio-ology?" he asked, his eyes as large as the proverbial saucers. She could see that he wasn't about to go along quietly until he understood where it was he was going to.

Kayley kept her answer simple. "That's just another name for the place where they're going to be taking pictures of your leg so that Dr. Dolan can fix it and make it all better."

Ralph appeared to respond to the promise of being "fixed."

"For real?" he asked, his voice hopeful.

"For real," Kayley assured him. "We just need to make one stop before we go down to the first floor, okay?"

Pressing his lips together bravely, Ralph surrendered a reluctant "Okay."

The stop that Kayley made was to her locker. She took out her headphones as well as the tablet that they were plugged into.

The white headphones were a source of curiosity for Ralph. "What's that?" he asked, eyeing them suspiciously.

"That's just something for you to use so that you can watch a movie on my tablet. It'll take your mind off the boring test," she told him. She waited for further questions, but for now, there were none. Putting out her hand to Ralph, she asked the jittery little boy, "Ready to get those pictures taken of your leg?"

He blew out a long, deep nervous breath, then reluctantly said, "I guess."

Because his injury made it difficult to walk, Kayley avoided the stairs and they took the elevator down to the medical building's first floor. Radiology was located directly opposite the elevator.

"What's that?" Ralph asked the moment they went through the doors and he heard a loud, rhythmic clunking noise. It sounded very much like a motor hitting the inside of a drainpipe.

Kayley explained without hesitation, "That's just the picture machine warming up."

She felt the boy tightening his fingers around her

hand. He seemed to shrink into her. "It's scary," he breathed.

"It's just a machine," she told him in a very calm, soothing voice. "It can't hurt you."

Ralph didn't look convinced.

And he looked even less so as they walked into the room where the MRI was located.

The technician, Teddy, glanced up when he heard them come in. "This the patient?" he asked, nodding toward the boy clinging to her.

"The one and only," Kayley answered. "This is Ralph Jordan. Ralph, this is Teddy, our super-smart MRI technician," she said, keeping her voice incredibly upbeat. "It's Teddy's job to make sure everything is running super smoothly. Okay, Ralph," she said, her smile never waning. "You're going to lie down on this table—" she pointed to it "—and the machine is going to take lots of pictures of your leg."

Ralph continued clutching on to her lab coat. He was looking at the table as if it were some sort of ancient sacrificial altar and it was his turn to be the new offering. He was practically shaking as he cried, "I don't want to lie down."

"You'll be doing me a really big favor if you do," Kayley said, gently prying his fingers from her coat, even as she allowed him to hang on to her hand. "It'll do all the work and take lots of pictures so the doctor can fix you all up to play soccer with your friends. You'll be good as new."

Ralph shook his head so hard his light brown hair flew back and forth about his face. "I changed my mind. I don't want to play soccer."

"But you want to walk, don't you, honey?" Kayley asked him in a voice that made it impossible for Ralph not to agree.

"Yeah, sure," he said, albeit a little leery.

"Well, the doctor needs to fix your leg so you can walk and he can't do that until he can see what's going on inside your leg. That means he needs those pictures from the MRI machine."

"Okay," he finally agreed.

Ralph let her help him onto the table, and then very gingerly, he lay down. But the moment he felt the table he was on begin to move and draw him into the machine—a lamb being slid into the mouth of the volcano—he began to scream and bolted upright.

Kayley signaled to the technician to stop. That was when she took out the headphones and tablet she'd thought to pick up on their way down here.

"Ralph, I want you to put these headphones on and just concentrate on the movie that you see on the tablet. Can you do that for me?" Kayley asked him.

The boy didn't appear too amenable, but Kayley had already pulled up the movie and he saw what was on the screen. It was an action flick depicting a group of popular superheroes joining forces to save the world.

Ralph complied and lay down quietly.

Kayley adjusted the headphones and gave it a few seconds. When she was fairly certain that the boy was completely captivated by what he saw on the tablet, she looked over toward Teddy and nodded at the technician.

"Go ahead," she told him. "I think Ralph'll be fine now."

Fortunately, the test required that only the boy's lower torso be inside the cylinder, leaving his upper torso and head free and clear of what was, for Ralph, obviously an extremely intimidating machine.

Kayley remained standing beside Ralph for the duration of the test, watching him to make sure that the tablet didn't suddenly lose its Wi-Fi connection for some reason, thereby possibly plunging the boy back into a state of terror.

"You want a chair?" the tech asked, raising his voice so she could hear him above the constant clatter of the machine.

Kayley would have preferred to be sitting, but she didn't want to risk any deviation from the procedure setting Ralph off. The sooner this test was over with, the sooner she could get the boy back upstairs and away from the frightening MRI machine.

The test took a total of forty-five minutes. Looking at Ralph's face told her that he had gotten comfortable lying here and watching the superheroes racing to save humanity on her tablet. He looked completely enthralled with the action on the screen, which was what she had been hoping for.

When the test was finally over, the table moved back into the neutral position where it had started. Ralph seemed surprised when she picked him up from the table and set him down on the floor.

His small face puckered up in consternation.

"That's it?" he asked when she took the headphones off his ears.

"That's it," she answered. "I told you that the test would go fast. Let's get you back upstairs to the exam room so your mom can find you when she gets back with your little brother."

"Can I watch the movie until she gets back?"

She smiled at Ralph fondly as she told him, "Sure."

"Cool," he responded, plopping the headphones back on his head. His eyes were immediately riveted on the action on the screen.

With a laugh, she guided him back onto the elevator and took him to the second floor.

As they got out of the elevator, Kayley put her hand on his shoulder and "steered" Ralph back to the original exam room.

Ralph never took his eyes off the tablet.

Happily for him, his mother returned with his little brother in tow just as the movie he was watching so intently came to an end.

Chapter Six

Kayley thought she was going to have to go looking for the doctor to tell him that Ralph's test was over. However, Luke walked into the exam room at almost the very same time that Mrs. Jordan and her younger son, Simon, did.

Ralph perked up as soon as he saw his mother. "I got to watch this really cool movie on Kayley's tablet," he told her excitedly. "Can we come back here again?" This time, the question was directed to Kayley, not his mother. His little brother instantly looked wistful, as if he was left out because he wanted to see a movie, too.

"I'm sure we're going to," his mother responded, glancing at the doctor to find out just what the next step was.

"I'll give you a call either late this afternoon or to-morrow morning, once I get a chance to review the MRI scans," Luke told her.

Janis Jordan nodded. Not knowing which of them had taken her son down for the test, Mrs. Jordan threw the question out to both of them.

"Did he give you any trouble?" It looked as if her younger son would cause her to lose her balance at any moment.

"Ralph was great," Kayley reassured the boy's mother.

Ralph was obviously eager to describe his experience. Words all but exploded from his lips.

"She put me on this table and it sounded like this giant machine was going to swallow me, but I wasn't scared, Mom." The eleven-year-old proudly puffed up his chest. "Kayley put these big headphones on me, you know, like Grandpa likes to listen to, and I couldn't hear the loud chomping noise the machine was making. All I heard was what the superheroes were saying."

Still being yanked to one side, Mrs. Jordan looked at her wearily and said a heartfelt "Thank you."

Kayley's genial smile filtered into her eyes as she told the woman, "Don't mention it. I'm just glad I could help so that he wasn't afraid."

"Afraid?" Ralph crowed as if that was the furthest thing from his mind. "I want to do it again." He turned around to look at Kayley and asked her, "Can we do it again?"

"We'll see. First we have to get you well," she said, putting her hand on his shoulder and guiding him to the door. "Now go home with your mom and help her out by being good, okay?"

"Okay," Ralph agreed brightly, clearly keen to please his new friend.

As the trio left the office, Kayley could almost feel

the doctor's eyes washing over her, taking measure of her as if she were some kind of alien creature.

"Headphones?" he asked.

She nodded, explaining, "I was trying to distract him."

Luke appeared to still be wrestling with the initial details. "You carry around headphones and some sort of a tablet with you?"

Evidently, the man wasn't one of those people who was attached to his wireless device. She wouldn't go so far as to say she was attached to hers, but she did like having it close by. And it had turned out to be handy this time around.

"It's a long story." One she was fairly confident that he didn't want her to get into. "But the point is it did work in this instance."

"Yes, I know." He saw her looking at him in surprise. He supposed that he could tell her he'd checked in on how things were going. "The technician said he would have had a hell of a time taking that MRI if you hadn't gotten the patient to watch some movie or other that you had on your tablet."

Ordinarily, he wasn't a curious man, but he had to admit, there were things about this woman that managed to arouse his curiosity.

"If you don't mind my asking, just how did you happen to have that particular movie available for the boy?"

It wasn't all that unique an occurrence. "I've got a lot of movies on my tablet." She smiled at the doctor, wondering what he would think of her when he heard her freely admit, "As it happens, I am a fan of superheroes. I have been ever since I was a little girl."

Maybe it was a female thing. "My daughter is, too," Luke told her, and then he had to qualify his statement. "I think."

Kayley cocked her head slightly to one side as she looked at him incredulously. "You think?" she repeated. "You don't know?"

He upbraided himself for saying anything, but he couldn't very well just walk out without appearing to be exceptionally rude.

"We don't exactly get much chance to talk," he told the overenergized physician's assistant. "She's asleep when I leave, and most of the time, she's asleep when I come home."

That didn't seem right. "How early is her bedtime?" Kayley questioned. "The office closes at five. I assume that you go home not too long after that."

"You assume wrong," Luke informed her. "After the office closes, I do evening rounds at the hospital, checking on all my patients who had inpatient surgery."

"Okay," Kayley allowed. "But that still leaves weekends."

"Not really," he answered. "I volunteer at a free clinic in Santa Ana on Saturdays and at another one in LA on Sundays."

Like a lightbulb that had been turned out, her bright smile faded and an expression that was half sad, half reproving took its place. He thought he even saw pity in her eyes, which irked him.

"You do realize that you're missing the best years of your daughter's life," Kayley pointed out.

He didn't care to be lectured to, especially not by a new hire. "We'll have time," Luke told the interfering woman curtly.

She knew she should keep her mouth shut, but Kayley couldn't help herself. The words just burst out before she could hold them back. The man was lucky enough to have a child and he seemed almost indifferent to the little girl.

"When?" she asked. "When you're walking her down the aisle at her wedding?"

His eyes narrowed. Obviously, Quartermain didn't understand that he was struggling to hold his tongue. "That is none of your business. You were hired to assist me in the exam rooms, Ms. Quartermain, not organize my personal life."

"On the contrary, Dr. Dolan, your personal life is very organized. Down to the split second. What you need is a little *dis*organization in your life. Specifically, some free time to spend with your daughter."

He wondered if the woman realized that she was inches away from being fired. This was still the trial period. "You're overstepping your place."

"Maybe," she agreed, and he thought that was the end of it. He should have realized that it wasn't. "But there's a little girl's happiness at stake. Now, I'm sure that your mother-in-law is really great with her, but a little girl *needs* her daddy. Heaven knows I would have given anything to have had some extra time with mine," she said with such heartfelt sincerity that it caught him totally unprepared for a moment.

Luke was the first one to admit that he wasn't good with emotional situations.

"Um, yes, well—" He had no idea what to say in the face of grief and loss, so after a moment spent being completely tongue-tied, he just switched topics. "Good job today with that boy."

Kayley's smile was back, although he noted that it was the tiniest bit frayed around the edges, as if she was putting him on notice that this discussion wasn't over with yet.

"Thank you, Doctor." And then she explained, "I just treated him the way I would have wanted to be treated at his age."

Luke was all set to retreat to his office, to remain there until office hours resumed at two, but her statement caught his interest as well as once again arousing his curiosity.

"You can remember that far back?" he asked, wondering if she was just putting him on. "That is, I don't mean to imply that you're anywhere near old, but there has to be about twenty years between you and that boy—"

"Twenty-one, actually," Kayley corrected.

"Okay," Luke said, accepting the number. "That makes it an even bigger difference in age. How can you *possibly* remember what it was like to be eleven?" he asked. He barely remembered what he'd done a week ago. She had to be pulling his leg.

To his surprise, Kayley said, "Easily. I remember being upset that nobody took the time to explain to me what was about to happen when I went in to get my tonsils out. I was always getting sick and coming down with a sore throat. And then suddenly, there I was, eight years old and in a hospital gown. My mother had to work, so she couldn't remain with me and I remember being totally terrified."

She was setting him up. This had to do with her lecture about practicing more personalized medicine, he was sure of it.

"Let me guess—a kindly old doctor sat down with you, explained everything, and suddenly, you weren't afraid anymore," he said sarcastically.

"You're only half-right," Kayley replied, ignoring his tone. "Actually, it was an intern. Dr. Greene. He was still in the formative stage and hadn't become jaded yet." She deliberately caught Luke's gaze. "He told me that there was nothing to be afraid of. That he had a little girl my age and she had just had the very same operation. Whether or not he was making it up, I don't know, but it really helped me at the time. I wasn't exactly blasé when I was taken into surgery, but I wasn't terrified anymore, either."

Luke gave her a very skeptical look. "And you're telling me this so I start holding my patients' hands and talking to them to make the surgical experience a pleasant experience for them?"

The man was being pigheaded—she could tell that by his tone of voice. Anything she said about the way he related to his patients would only get him to dig his heels in more.

"I wouldn't presume to tell you what to do with your patients, Doctor. That's for you to decide. But I really would suggest that you find a little bit of time for your daughter before she's grown and going away to college. Except when you're sitting in a dentist's chair getting a root canal, time really does move very fast, and before you know it, it's gone."

What she said struck home, even though he didn't want to admit it. It didn't make him think about the dentist, but it did make him think of Jill. He'd been so convinced that they had all the time in the world. That they'd grow old together and have time to travel as a couple rather than having half a world between them, with her at home while he was overseas.

Kayley saw the expression on his face change. Either she had managed to get him to come around a little…or she was going to be fired by the end of the day. Still, she didn't regret what she had just said to him. If anything, she regretted not being able to get through to him.

"Don't forget to take that box of doughnuts for Lily and your mother-in-law home," she told Luke just before she made herself scarce.

Walking into his office, Luke sat down and then glanced at his schedule. His last inpatient was scheduled to be released once he checked the man over.

He supposed that there was no law that said he had to do it after his office hours. He knew the hospital actually preferred patients going home earlier than later. The rule of thumb had always been to make them well and get them on their feet, moving toward home. As quickly as possible.

If he signed Elliot Murphy out now, before office hours resumed this afternoon—and didn't stay after hours to review his files and the surgeries he had scheduled for tomorrow—he could get home before Lily's bedtime.

The thought of seeing his daughter made his stomach tighten just a little.

Luke had to admit to himself that he was keeping these long hours in part to avoid being around Lily. She looked like a miniature of her mother, so much so that it sometimes *hurt* to look at her.

But more than that, he had to come to grips with

the fact that he just didn't know how to relate to a five-year-old.

He supposed it came back to his lack of people skills, the thing that this new PA kept harping on. Lord, but he missed Jill. He hadn't needed people skills with Jill. She'd talked for the both of them and seemed to intuit what he was thinking. He hadn't really needed to say much of anything. She'd known him inside and out.

He rose to his feet. Maybe that annoying physician's assistant with that wide smile had a point. Maybe it was time for him to stop running like this and be grateful for what he did have before he didn't have that, either.

But first, there was a patient he needed to discharge from the hospital.

"Luke, is that you?" Barbara Baxter looked up, surprised and caught off guard when her son-in-law walked in through the front door at five minutes after six o'clock.

"Who did you think it was, a burglar with a key?" Luke quipped, resting his briefcase on the hall table.

Lily had bounced up from the sofa to see what the excitement was all about. She looked uncertainly at her father, not knowing what she was supposed to do.

"What's a burglar, Grandma?" she asked.

Not wanting to alarm the little girl, Barbara answered, "Someone coming in who you weren't expecting to be in your house."

"You mean like Daddy?" Lily asked, still looking at her father as if she thought perhaps she was just imagining him.

"Out of the mouths of babes," Barbara commented,

then waved Lily toward her father. "Go give your daddy a hug, honey."

Lily hung back, watching her father shyly.

She was small for her age and he towered over her. He supposed that he might look a little frightening to her. Kayley was right, he thought grudgingly. He needed to get home at a decent hour more often. It was as if Lily barely recognized him. If he kept this up, in another six months, she was liable not to know him at all.

"What's that?" she asked, pointing at the small bakery box in his hand.

He'd forgotten all about that. Holding it out to Lily, he said, "I brought you doughnuts."

She stared at him as if he had just told her he was one of the princes in the fairy tales he knew that Barbara read to her at bedtime.

"Really?" she asked in disbelief, rocking back and forth on her toes.

He glanced at his mother-in-law for confirmation as he added, "With rainbow sprinkles."

"Rainbow sprinkles? Can I see?" Lily asked excitedly. Then, as if there were any doubt about her being able to accept the dessert, she told him, "I ate my dinner."

Because he left everything up to his mother-in-law—just as he had with Jill—and she was rearing Lily in his place, he looked at the woman to give Lily the go-ahead. "Barbara?" he asked.

"Don't look at me," she said, shooing him away. "Bond with your daughter."

He opened the box, allowing both his daughter and his mother-in-law to see its contents.

Noticing the jelly doughnut nestled beside the two with rainbow sprinkles, Barbara reached in and plucked it out of the box.

"Lucas, are you bonding with me?" she asked, holding the doughnut up like a trophy. Powdered sugar rained down, leaving a slight confectionary trail in its wake.

"The doughnuts are from my physician's assistant," he told both of them, wanting to take no false credit for how the treats happened to have found their way into his house.

"You mean Kayley?" Barbara asked, remembering the young woman who had called on the phone. "It's been ages since I had one of these," she told Luke, taking a bite of the pastry and savoring the taste. "I am beginning to like that girl more and more, Luke."

He frowned. "That makes one of us."

"I like her, too," Lily declared just before she stuffed half a doughnut into her small mouth.

Maybe he should have gone with tradition and released his patient after office hours after all, Luke thought, feeling somewhat awkward.

Chapter Seven

Luke started skipping his lunches. Rather than staying in his office and ordering in, he used the time between noon and two, when the office was closed, to go across the street to the hospital and check on the handful of inpatients he had. If any of them were to be discharged that day, he did it at that time instead of at the end of the day.

So, barring the occasional emergency that required his attention in the ER when he was on call, Luke was able to get home somewhere around six o'clock.

Things still were somewhat awkward and strained between Lily and him, but he felt that they were getting less so, bit by bit. The little girl was opening up to him and he was trying to do the same with her. This was what Jill would have wanted.

And if he was being entirely honest with himself, it was what he wanted, as well.

But it took work. More work than he would have thought. He supposed that just went along with the old adage that anything worthwhile always required a great deal of effort. Lily had been little more than a toddler, barely two, when he'd left for duty overseas. And then he'd been gone for two years. It was no wonder that his daughter looked upon him as a stranger— just a man she'd seen in the pictures her mother had shown her and an occasional voice on the phone.

Lily smiled at him now when he came home. And sometimes she even hugged him. Not with the abandon typical of a child her age, but cautiously, like she was anticipating rejection on some level.

That needed work, but it was ultimately his fault and he accepted the full blame. He also accepted the fact that it was up to him to do the work until the situation improved.

To that end, he was happy that he no longer looked at Lily and saw only Jill in her. He was beginning to recognize a little of himself within his daughter, as well.

Establishing a relationship with Lily was a work in progress, Luke told himself, trying to focus on the word *progress*.

When he walked in on Kayley in one of the recently vacated exam rooms a few weeks later, she was just terminating the call she was on. There was a strange expression on her face—like someone getting caught doing what she wasn't supposed to be doing.

He found that his curiosity was piqued. "Something wrong?" Luke asked.

Kayley looked at her phone before tucking it away

and took a deep breath. "That all depends on your point of view, I guess."

"You don't have to tell me," he said dismissively, feeling uncomfortable. "I was only making conversation." He changed topics. "Apparently, according to Julia," he said, referring to one of the administrative assistants at the front desk, "Mr. Jacobson canceled his two-o'clock appointment for today, so we have some extra downtime. If you'd like to take a longer lunch today, feel free to do so."

Preoccupied before, Kayley became alert. "As a matter of fact, I could use the extra time."

"Well then, it all worked out, didn't it?" he said rather formally. He was already walking away from the exam room.

Kayley took a step after him, wanting to ask a question before he disappeared on her. "You wouldn't know your daughter's favorite cake, would you?"

Now what was the woman up to? Luke turned around to look at her. "Why?"

"Well, it's always polite to bring something when you're invited to dinner," Kayley began to explain, knowing that she was starting in the middle rather than at the beginning. But she never knew just how the doctor was going to take something and she wanted to ease into the subject slowly. However, she was hampered by the fact that she didn't have all that much time to get her information.

"Are you having dinner with my daughter?" he asked.

Was *that* why she had looked so confused when he'd walked in on her? But Lily had just turned five years old. Five-year-olds didn't make arrangements for dinner. What was going on here?

Kayley hesitated, searching for a way to frame her reply without setting the doctor off. "I think you should be forewarned."

"About what?" Luke asked, his voice sounding dangerously low.

Kayley took a breath before answering. "Your mother-in-law invited me for dinner."

He knew that Barbara still owned that condo she'd lived in before Jill's death. She'd bought it shortly before Lily was born so she could help Jill out with the baby occasionally. The condo was located in Bedford, near the university.

After Jill's death, his mother-in-law had moved into his house so she could help him take care of Lily. Oh, who was he kidding? She'd moved in to take over raising the little girl while he tried to rebuild his life and find a way to go on with his work.

His eyes locked with Kayley's. "At her place?" he asked.

She supposed anywhere a person resided could be referred to as their place. "In a manner of speaking, yes."

"Out with it, Quartermain. You're usually very vocal—about *everything*. What is it you're trying to say this time?" he asked.

This was *not* of her doing; however, she supposed she had no choice but to spit it out. "That was your mother-in-law on the phone just now. She asked me to come to dinner. The way she made it sound, dinner was at your house. With Lily."

Kayley assumed since he'd been going home at an

incredibly decent hour, that he would be there, as well. She felt it only fair to let him know about his mother-in-law's invitation before he walked in and found her seated at his table. "I know that it's rather unusual—"

"So, apparently, are you and my mother-in-law." Looking far from happy, Luke sighed. "What did you tell her?"

"I told her yes," she answered, still not taking her eyes off his face. Part of her was waiting for it to turn a bright shade of red. She began to reach for her cell phone again. "I'll call her to cancel if you'd rather I didn't come."

"I have no feelings about this one way or another," he told her brusquely, which wasn't altogether true.

The idea of sharing a meal with her was both somewhat intriguing as well as just the tiniest bit disconcerting. As for it coming from Barbara, he didn't want his PA getting the wrong idea. The invitation was just to satisfy his mother-in-law's curiosity. And possibly, she was trying to do the same for Lily, who had ventured a couple of questions about the woman who had sent her doughnuts.

His laser-like scrutiny was making her uncomfortable. "So it's all right with you if I come over?"

Broad shoulders rose and fell beneath a starched white lab coat. "Like I said, it doesn't matter to me. I won't be there tonight, anyway." He had a late discharge that he hadn't been able to work in at noon. The woman had needed a couple of tests to be processed before she could be discharged and that wasn't happening until after two at the earliest.

"It's not for tonight," Kayley told him. "It's for tomorrow night."

"Saturday," he acknowledged. "Well, I'm at the clinic."

"Actually, tomorrow is your alternate Saturday," she reminded him rather gently. "Dr. Barnett takes over for you every other Saturday."

He frowned. He didn't like being wrong, or corrected. Most of all, he didn't like being backed up into a corner, which was what he felt his mother-in-law was doing.

"How is it you know my schedule better than I do?" Luke asked gruffly.

"Because I'm efficient and that's part of what you pay me for," she answered guilelessly. Debating for a moment—because she really did want to come to dinner—she finally told him, "I'll call Mrs. Baxter back and tell her that I can't come."

"No, you can't do that," he told her gruffly. "She'll think I forced you to say that. Barbara's a good woman, but she can make her displeasure known in a hundred small, subtle ways that can make life turn into a living hell. In the long run, agreeing to this dinner is the easier option."

Kayley turned her brilliant smile on him. "As long as it's all right with you."

No, it's not all right with me, he thought, doing his best not to be mesmerized by that smile of hers. *It's not all right, because you've already infiltrated my professional life enough. I don't want to be looking at you across a table in my own house.*

But he knew that it was something he was better off temporarily coming to terms with. Besides, with both Barbara and Lily there, he wouldn't be required to contribute one word to the conversation.

Even so, there was one conversation that he most certainly intended to have, however fleeting it might turn out to be.

"Don't you think that you should have run asking my physician's assistant to dinner by me first?" Luke asked his mother-in-law the moment he walked into the house that night.

Instead of answering his question, Barbara told him, "Lily missed you at dinner tonight."

He sincerely doubted that. He hadn't been coming home for dinner that much since he'd returned from the fighting overseas. Definitely not often enough for the little girl to become accustomed to seeing him there.

"No, she didn't," he told Barbara firmly, "and besides, it couldn't have been avoided." He frowned, giving her a look that said he knew what she was up to. "You're changing the subject, Barbara."

Her smile was quick and spasmodic. "Sorry, I learned that from the master," she told him, and there was no mistaking who she meant by that.

"That 'master' is turning the question back to you," Luke informed her. This time his voice was steely as he repeated his questions. "Why didn't you ask me if it was all right before you invited Quartermain to dinner?"

"Because you would have said no."

He saw no reason to deny it. "I see that woman enough five days a week at work."

"Well, that's beside the point. I wanted to meet the woman who got you to bring home a box of doughnuts to Lily and to me."

Why was she making that big a deal out of it? Barbara was well-off enough to have bought and sold the entire bakery. "It was only three doughnuts."

"Still, you had never done that before," Barbara reminded him. "And I wanted to meet her for other reasons."

"What reasons?" he asked suspiciously.

"Admit it—Kayley is the one who got you to finally come home at a decent hour and to alternate Saturdays and Sundays at the clinic with other doctors. If you ask me, that is a very persuasive, impressive young woman."

"I didn't ask," he told her.

Barbara knew and liked her former son-in-law and she understood this blustery exterior that he had erected between himself and the world ever since Jill had died. Knew and understood but didn't condone. Right now she felt that he was only half-alive and his daughter needed him to be fully committed to life.

"I still stand by my assessment," she told him mildly.

He tried to appeal to her from a different angle. "Barbara, I've never had any of the other staff over for dinner."

"And whose fault is that, Lucas?" she asked him lightly.

"Why is there this sudden desire to turn me into a social creature?" he asked, feeling irritated and stymied.

"Because charm like yours shouldn't be hidden from the world," she told him drily. "Look, Lucas," Barbara said in a far more serious tone. "Working yourself to death and hiding in the off moments isn't going to change anything. Much as it pains me to say it, doing what you're doing isn't going to bring Jill back. And Jill wouldn't want you living like Rasputin."

Now the woman had completely lost him. "Come again?" he asked.

"Rasputin," she repeated, then explained, "The mad monk."

"I know who Rasputin is," he said, exasperated. "What I don't know is what are you up to?"

"Just trying to get you socialized, and starting with the woman who actually seems to have made some sort of headway with you in regards to that. She got you to bring doughnuts to your daughter—and to me. And she got you to come home once in a while. A woman like that is a woman I really want to meet." She looked at him innocently. "There's nothing wrong with that."

"There is if you drag me in on it."

"I've got news for you," Barbara said, patting his cheek. "You're already dragged into it. Now stop complaining and deal with it, Lucas. Tomorrow evening is going to make your daughter very happy. She seems to regard Kayley as her heroine."

How did all this happen? Luke wondered, stunned. "Quartermain is not—"

"And try not to call her by her last name like that, Lucas. She's your physician's assistant. You work together—you're not inhabiting a marine trench together."

"I guess you're right about that," Luke agreed. "If I were in a trench, I'd have a fighting chance of getting out alive."

Barbara sighed, shaking her head. "Is this what my daughter had to put up with? This spirit-drowning pessimism of yours? Jill was a braver girl than I realized."

He frowned at her. He knew she meant well, but that still didn't change the bottom line. Quartermain was breaching his private domain by coming over for dinner tomorrow night.

"You still should have asked me," he told her.

"Next time," Barbara replied cheerfully. "By the way, if you're hungry, Lily left you some dinner on the stove. Not really sure what it is," she confessed. "She insisted on preparing something for you by herself."

"You let her cook?" he asked, wondering if his mother-in-law had lost her mind.

"I let her put together bread and cold cuts. No lit matches were involved. Now, if you don't mind, arguing always tires me out," she said, turning toward the rear of the house, where her bedroom was. "I'm going to bed."

"Bed?" he echoed. "It's only—" He had to pause as he looked around for a clock.

"Late," Barbara called over her shoulder. "It's actually later than you think, Lucas."

He wanted to ask her what she meant by that, but he knew it would only lead them into an argument and even though her actions today had annoyed him, he owed his mother-in-law a great deal. He would have been hard-pressed dealing with Lily and juggling her care with his practice, especially feeling the way that he did. Right now being a doctor was what he was. He needed that to tether him to life and he had a feeling that in her own way, Barbara understood that. Understood it and did what she could to facilitate things so that he could go on practicing, go on making a difference.

Some days he won. Other days his demons did. But

without Barbara being there to take care of Lily, the demons would have won a lot more days than they had. Possibly all of them by now.

Opening the refrigerator, he found a large, rather sloppy sandwich on a plate. There was a note attached with tape to the plate. It read "Daddy's dinner" in big sprawling block letters.

Touched, he brought it over to the kitchen table. He sat and ate the sandwich slowly.

He discovered that smiling made it more difficult to chew.

Chapter Eight

Saturday morning Barbara knocked on the door leading into the den and silently counted to ten before knocking one more time. She knew that Luke usually got so involved in whatever he was doing he didn't hear anything. She also knew that if he wasn't at the hospital or in his office, he would be in his den, reading up on the latest orthopedic surgical procedures.

She was about to knock one last time when she heard Luke speak up from inside the den.

"Come in."

Her hand on the doorknob, she opened it only far enough to peer into the room. "I just wanted to remind you that dinner is going to be at five, Lucas. I trust you're planning to be here," Barbara told him pointedly.

His eyes met hers. He still wasn't 100 percent sure about dinner tonight. He was certainly undecided about the wisdom of doing this.

"I'm a doctor, Barbara. That means I'm on call twenty-four hours a day," he reminded her.

"Well, actually, you're not," Barbara contradicted. "I spoke with Stephen Barrett and he agreed to take any of your calls should an emergency come up."

"He agreed?" Luke asked incredulously. He didn't know whether to be angry or impressed. For the moment, he just tried to keep his cool, and then he asked, "How did you manage that?"

Barbara smiled in satisfaction. "You forget that my husband didn't just act as your mentor. There's a whole legion of doctors that Dan trained. A few of them are in your orthopedic medical group. All I had to do was mention his name and Stephen was more than happy to step in as your substitute if the need arises."

His eyes narrowed. "You didn't happen to tell him why you were asking him to be on call, did you?"

Barbara gave him a reproachful look. "I'm not senile yet, Lucas. I just said something had come up. Vague enough for you?" she asked.

"Yes."

It was a grudging acknowledgment but it *was* an acknowledgment. "And if you have any thoughts about ducking out at the last minute, I would advise against it."

He'd thought about it, but he didn't want to put his mother-in-law on the spot, even though she apparently had no such compunctions in regards to putting him on the spot, he thought.

"Is that why you're having dinner at five?" he asked her.

She nodded. "That and Lily wants to be there. She gets very tired around seven. This way she can visit for a little while before it's her bedtime." Again, Barbara looked at him pointedly. "She's really looking forward to meeting 'the doughnut lady.' By the way, it's a lovely day. Why don't you go outside and take advantage of it by doing something with Lily?"

He had no idea how to "do something" with Lily. Luke suppressed a sigh. He was outmaneuvered and outnumbered. He felt like a fish caught on a hook. The more he thrashed, the worse it seemed to be for him. So he resigned himself to the situation—although if the occasion presented itself for him to successfully duck out, he still might, he told himself.

The thought of ducking out became more enticing as the morning wore on, giving way to the afternoon. As he was seriously considering taking a ride somewhere just for the sheer novelty of it, his path to the car was blocked by just over three and a half feet of determined little girl.

As he looked down into Lily's face, it struck him that she definitely had something on her mind. Something that would make him feel like a fish out of water.

"Lily, why don't you help Grandma get dinner ready for your guest?" he suggested.

"Grandma doesn't want any help," Lily answered without any hesitation. "She says she's got everything under control." Lily cocked her head much the way he'd noticed Quartermain doing about a week ago. Maybe it was a quirk common to stubborn women, regardless of their age. "She said that you could help me."

Lily had never sought him out for anything before. He couldn't very well turn her away now, but he also wasn't very good when it came to the things that little girls were into.

"Help you with what?" Luke asked his daughter gamely.

Raising her chin and looking very determined, Lily said, "I wanted to give the lady who's coming to dinner something special."

"That's nice." He nodded absently. "You mean like a drawing?" he asked.

The look on the small oval face bordered on impatience. "No, everybody can do a drawing," she said, then told him, "I want to give her a leprechaun."

Luke congratulated himself on not laughing out loud. Instead, he merely repeated, "A leprechaun."

Lily bobbed her head up and down with the energy and enthusiasm that was the exclusive property of the very young and idealistic.

Luke continued to play along. "Do you happen to have a leprechaun lying around somewhere?"

"No, silly. Leprechauns don't just lie around," Lily giggled.

It was the first time that he recalled ever hearing her giggle and the sound captivated him. And perhaps, for the first time, he was beginning to see her as an individual, not just a little girl who was a carbon copy of so many other little girls.

"We have to catch one," Lily told her father.

"And how do you suggest we do that?" he asked her, curious to hear if she had this all worked out or if this was the part where she just handed the problem over to him and waited for him to come up with a plan.

Apparently, he learned, Lily had it all worked out. "We build a box and draw a rainbow inside of it. And maybe we put a piece of gold in front of the rainbow. Leprechauns like gold," she informed him assertively. "We tie a piece of string to the box and once he goes inside it to get the gold, we pull the string. Bang!" she declared proudly. "The box goes down and we've caught a leprechaun."

Luke laughed, charmed. He shook his head in disbelief. That was a pretty sophisticated plan for a five-year-old, he couldn't help thinking. "You really do have all this worked out, don't you?"

She bobbed her head up and down, golden curls bouncing back and forth. "Uh-huh. Grandma says, 'Do it right, or don't do it at all,'" she told him, deepening her voice to imitate her grandmother.

Luke nodded, trying to look solemn. He was doing his best not to laugh again.

"That certainly does sound just like her," Luke agreed.

She was still staring up at him, her eyes wide and beseeching. "So will you help me?"

How could he say no to that face? So, nodding, he said, "I guess we'd better get started, then."

Deep blue eyes softened around the edges as a smile curved the small rosebud mouth. "Then you'll build me a box? Grandma says there's some wood, a hammer and some nails in the garage."

No longer shy and now on a mission, Lily took his hand in her tiny one and tugged on it, beginning to lead him into the garage.

"Okay."

This sounded much too easy and smelled like a setup, he thought. Following Lily into the garage, he saw the wood.

The planks were all different sizes, leftovers from some project. Whose, he hadn't a clue, although he vaguely recalled that Jill had once taken a wood-working class because she'd thought it was a good way to distract herself while he was in medical school.

That was a long time ago, he thought, trying to keep the memory and everything it conjured up at bay. The wood was probably rotten.

To his surprise, the wood turned out to be all right. As a matter of fact, it was more than all right. It was of a high-grade quality.

But, high-grade quality or not, the planks weren't going to do him any good if he couldn't find a way to cut them down to one uniform size.

Putting five planks down on the workbench, he glanced around the garage. "Lily, you wouldn't hap-pen to know if there's a saw around here, do—"

He didn't get a chance to finish his question. His daughter ran over to what turned out to be a tool rack and then pointed. Someone had taught her to keep a respectful distance away from anything that could ac-cidentally hurt her.

Crossing to where Lily was standing, Luke felt a wistful pang in the center of his gut.

You did a great job with her, Jill. And you did it all without me, he thought.

He was a highly skilled, very respected surgeon. However, that did him no good when it came to being a handyman. That meant that cutting five equal pieces of wood and then hammering them all together to form a makeshift box in order to capture a mythical lepre-chaun was not exactly easy.

The hardest part, though, was not letting loose with

a string of choice words when he missed the nail and hit his thumb instead—not once but a total of three different times.

The third time, he hit it so hard that strong tears sprang to his eyes.

That was when Lily slid off the stool she'd been sitting on and, taking his hand in hers, surprised him by bringing his thumb up to her lips and giving it such a gentle kiss it made him think of a butterfly fluttering down and lightly perching on the petal of a flower.

She was a sweetheart, he thought.

"There," she pronounced, letting his hand go and stepping back. "Whenever I had a boo-boo, Mommy would kiss it to make it all better." Big blue eyes looked up at him. "Is it all better, Daddy?"

It would be wonderful if everything were just this simple. Out loud, he told her, "It's good as new."

Her small face puckered up as she tried to understand. "Then why are there still tears in your eyes?" she asked.

"Must be the dust in the air," he said. He took his handkerchief out and proceeded to elaborately wipe the "dust" away.

Tucking his handkerchief back into his pocket, he got back to work.

"There—it's done," he declared several minutes later.

"Not yet," she told him. He looked at her quizzically. "Don't forget the nail for the string," she reminded him, sounding exactly like a little old lady. "Without the string, we can't pull down the box and the leprechaun will get away."

"Certainly can't have that," Luke agreed.

He drove a nail into the front of the small wooden box and attached a string to it, then tied the string tightly around the nail.

"Don't forget, we need a rainbow," he noted. "Do you need a piece of paper and a box of crayons?" he asked.

"Already got 'em," she said. "The rainbow will be ready in a jiffy," she promised. Armed with her "tools," Lily plopped down, tummy first, onto the floor and threw herself into the job.

It took her only a few minutes to draw the all-important rainbow. Stopping, she critically surveyed her creation before retiring the crayons back into the box. He caught himself thinking that she had to be the neatest five-year-old ever created.

"Finished!" she announced, holding out her work of art.

Taking the drawing from her, he was surprised to see that it looked a lot better than he'd expected. Most children in kindergarten drew things that resembled a mass of scribbles. Lily's rainbow actually looked like a rainbow.

The colors ran together a little here and there, but for the most part, it was a rainbow that was "guaranteed to fool any leprechaun," he assured her.

"We still need a piece of gold," he told his daughter, thinking that would be a sticking point. "And I'm afraid that I—"

Again, he didn't get a chance to finish.

Lily dug into her pocket, then held up something in the palm of her hand.

"Will this do?" she asked innocently.

It wasn't gold, although the coin was gold in color.

What she showed him was a one-dollar coin minted in 2000 honoring the Native American guide who had taken Lewis and Clark to the Pacific coast.

"Where did you get that?" he asked.

"Grandma gave it to me when I told her I wanted to capture a leprechaun and I needed some gold. Will it work?"

So Barbara was in on this. He should have known.

Luke nodded. "The leprechaun will never know the difference," he assured her.

Luke watched her eyes sparkle, and to his amazement, he found himself suddenly falling in love with a five-year-old.

"Well, I guess we'd better get this set up. Do you want this in the front yard or the back?" he asked Lily since this was clearly her safari.

She never even stopped to think.

"Front," she answered with unwavering conviction. "Leprechauns don't like backyards. They like big open spaces so they can escape really fast if they have to."

Luke smiled warmly at the imaginative little girl. "And how do you know all this?"

"Mommy told me," she said solemnly. "And then Grandma read this story to me about leprechauns and how smart they are."

Luke nodded. "They are, you know," he concurred, getting completely into the spirit of this venture. He thought this was as good a time as any to warn his creative daughter, "So we might not catch one today even after all your hard work."

She surprised him with the degree of maturity in her voice as she answered, "I know, Daddy. But it's the thought that counts and the doughnut lady will know I was thinking about her when I did this."

"I'll be sure to tell her if she doesn't figure it out on her own," Luke promised.

Lily's eyes crinkled as she smiled at him. "Thank you, Daddy."

He felt something really strong grip his heart. "My pleasure, Lily," he told her as solemnly as a knight speaking to his lady just as he was about to ride off into battle.

After walking around to the front lawn with Lily beside him, he placed the box on its side so that she could tape her drawing of the rainbow inside. Propping it up on a stick in order to allow the rainbow to be seen, he held the box steady so that she could put the "gold coin" meant to tempt the leprechaun on the grass.

All that remained after that was to run the length of string as far as it would go and then wait for the leprechaun to make his appearance.

Lily, he discovered, had a great deal of patience as she waited for the mythical little man in green to show up. He expected her to grow tired of the game in half an hour if not sooner, but she lasted a lot longer than that. Her perfect little face appeared solemn as she watched the mouth of the box, ready to pull the string should the leprechaun put in an appearance and venture inside the box to claim his "gold."

She was so intent on capturing a leprechaun that Luke found himself wishing there were some way to make the mythical creature appear, just for a moment. He couldn't help thinking that such dedication and perseverance should be rewarded.

* * *

Kayley realized she had driven right by the house. She'd been glancing at the addresses painted on the curb as she passed each of the homes on the residential through street. She didn't bother looking at the address of the house where a little girl was intently working on something with her father, because it never occurred to her, despite the fact that Dr. Dolan had a daughter, that *he* would be doing something with her like a typical father. There was nothing about Dolan that was typical.

Realizing her mistake, she drove down the block, turned around and made her way back. Playing it safe—what if she was wrong?—she parked across the street from the father and daughter in question. She got out and cautiously made her way across the street, watching the duo the entire time.

That *was* Dr. Dolan.

There were obviously things about her employer that she didn't know, Kayley thought with an amused smile.

They seemed completely oblivious to her until she was right behind them.

"What are you doing?"

The melodic voice coming from behind pierced the bubble around Lily and him, startling him.

Feeling like an idiot, Luke jumped to his feet even before the voice had fully registered and he'd realized that the question was coming from Kayley, who had managed to draw close without either of them hearing her.

Lily came to life immediately. "We're waiting for a leprechaun. Daddy built the box and we were going to trap him and give him to you as a present," Lily said excitedly.

"Really?" Kayley cried with the same enthusiasm that Lily had used. She slanted a glance toward Luke, humor shining in her eyes. "Well, that has to be the nicest 'almost present' anyone ever thought about giving me," she told the little girl. "I am really touched. Thank you."

Kayley put her arms around Lily, giving the little girl a warm hug. Rather than pull away, the way he'd expected her to, his daughter melted against her, threading her small arms around her legs.

"You're welcome," Lily said, her voice slightly muffled against Kayley's body. Tilting her head back, she told the woman, "Daddy worked hard on this, too. You can hug him if you want."

Yes, I 'want' but I think that might just throw your Daddy off if I did.

But, to her surprise—and quite possibly his, too—Lily tugged on her father's hand and brought him over toward her so that he could carry out the hug the girl had verbally set up for them.

Given no choice in the matter, Kayley went through the motions of hugging Lily's father.

"Thank you for my almost gift," she murmured.

"Don't mention it. Please," he underscored, stepping back. It almost sounded like an order.

Chapter Nine

"Well, what's all this?" Barbara asked with a delighted laugh.

She'd been drawn out by the commotion she heard coming from in front of the house, wondering what her granddaughter and her son-in-law were up to. This had to be a first. Ordinarily, Luke didn't interact with his daughter beyond exchanging a few words at the dinner table. That he appeared to be doing a project with her was heartwarming.

"Daddy and I tried to catch a leprechaun as a present for the doughnut lady," Lily told her, speaking up. "But the leprechaun hasn't come yet even though I made a rainbow for him. We put out some gold for him, too. Do you think he's sick?" Lily asked, concerned.

"He must be, to pass up a rainbow *and* gold," Barbara told her. Tickled, she looked at the woman standing between her granddaughter and Luke. "You must be Kayley," she concluded warmly.

Kayley put her hand out toward the older woman. "And you must be Mrs. Baxter," she surmised. "So good to finally meet you."

Barbara ignored the hand and drew the woman into a welcoming embrace.

"My sentiments exactly. And call me Barbara, please." Releasing her, Barbara looked at her son-in-law. "Luke, why didn't you bring Kayley in?" She turned toward the young woman and hooked her arm through Kayley's. "You have to forgive Lucas. He is a brilliant orthopedic surgeon, best in his field, bar none, but he's a bit lacking when it comes to people skills."

"I hadn't noticed," Kayley replied.

From the tone of her voice, it was hard for Barbara to determine whether she was kidding or serious.

Lily took the opportunity to grab hold of Kayley's hand. Tugging, the little girl began to lead her into the house.

"I'll take her in, Grandma!" she declared and proceeded to do just that. Eyeing the pink box in her guest's hand as they came in, she cried, "Are there doughnuts in that box?"

"Lily," Barbara admonished, coming in behind her.

"Actually, I brought a cake this time," Kayley told Lily. "Tiramisu," she specified.

Lily wrinkled her brow at the brand-new unknown word. "Terri-meow? What's that?"

Kayley tried to think of a way to describe the cake to the girl. "Do you like chocolate and cream?" she asked.

Lily nodded her head up and down so hard it looked as if it was in danger of coming right off. "Oh yes!"

Kayley smiled at the enthusiasm Lily displayed. "Then you're going to love tiramisu," she promised.

Lily's blue eyes fairly gleamed. "Okay," she answered with excited anticipation.

"All right, everyone, take your seats, please. Dinner is ready," Barbara announced.

Rather than the awkward conversation interwoven with equally awkward silences that Luke had expected at dinner, in the capable hands of his mother-in-law, his daughter and his physician's assistant, the discussion sped comfortably along without a single lull and barely a pause to allow for the intake of breath.

Barbara nudged him under the table with her foot not once but several times and nothing happened. The expression on his face told her that he knew what she was doing but he chose to simply hang back and listen rather than participate in a conversation that was racing along at a sixty-five-mile-an-hour clip without him.

Barbara gave him a reproving look but refrained from verbally admonishing him.

Eventually, Kayley leaned back from the table, so stuffed she was afraid she was going to explode. "That had to be one of the best meals I've had in a very long time," Kayley told the woman who had extended the invitation to her in the first place.

Barbara appeared exceptionally pleased by the compliment. "Then we definitely need to have you over more often," Barbara told her.

Kayley slid a glance toward the man she worked

for, fully anticipating that he would be red in the face from holding his peace right about now.

"I think the doctor sees enough of me around the office," she said, politely turning down the idea of another invitation.

"I doubt that, but even so, the invitation doesn't come from him," Barbara informed the younger woman. "It comes from me—"

"And me!" Lily cried, exuberantly joining in. "And maybe you can bring some more terri-meow cake."

"Tiramisu," Luke corrected.

Well, it was nice to know that he could still speak, Kayley thought. "Actually, I think I like her way better," she said, laughing and giving the little girl who'd been seated next to her a hug.

The next moment, Kayley rose from her chair.

"You're not leaving, are you?" Barbara asked, surprised by this sudden movement.

"Oh no," Kayley assured her hostess, realizing how this had to look to the older woman. She glanced around at the plates, which contained just the barest of remnants from the dinner. "I'm just clearing the table."

"You'll do no such thing," Barbara protested, rising to her feet herself.

"Since you did the cooking, it only seems fair that I take care of the cleanup," Kayley told her. When Barbara made no move to sit down, Kayley tried again. "Please sit. It'll make me feel better."

"You might as well give in, Barbara," Luke said. "I've learned that Kayley is exceedingly stubborn. She won't stop until she wears you down and wins."

But Barbara wasn't a pushover herself. She was not about to give in that easily. "My house, my rules, my dear. Now you three go out into the living room and enjoy yourselves," she instructed, waving them away from the dining room table. "I find the sound of Lily's laughter refreshing."

Seeing as how the older woman was determined to have her way, Kayley didn't want to insult Luke's former mother-in-law by arguing with her. In addition, she reminded Kayley too much of her late mother and there had never been a single argument between them.

"Luke?" Barbara said in a voice that he was well acquainted with. It said she expected no further resistance from either of them.

"Lily, take Ms. Quartermain into the living room. I'll be right there. I need a minute with Grandma," he told his daughter.

"Who's Ms. Quarter-something?" Lily asked, completely bewildered.

"That's me," Kayley told the little girl. She bent closer to Lily. "But you can call me Kayley." She winked at the five-year-old. "It's easier."

Completely won over, Lily cried, "Okay," then took Kayley's hand in hers and led her into the other room, just as her grandmother had said.

Barbara waited until her granddaughter and their guest were out of earshot before she turned toward her son-in-law. "Lucas, I'm in no mood for a lecture," she warned him.

"No lectures," he replied as he began to mechanically help her clear the table. "But I do have a question for you."

Barbara paused, bracing herself. "All right, Lucas. Go ahead."

"'My house, my rules'?" he repeated, obviously questioning her use of the phrase.

"Technically, it's your house," Barbara allowed. "But you did ask me to move in with you, so that makes it my house, as well," she pointed out. Looking at her son-in-law knowingly, she said, "Now stop stalling and get out there and keep our guest company."

Instead of doing as she asked, Luke continued clearing the table. He carried the near-empty side plates and bread basket out to the kitchen counter. "I'm sure that Lily can adequately fill that position," he told Barbara.

"I know that she can," Barbara said without any hesitation. "But it's getting close to Lily's bedtime," she reminded him. "Now go out there and be the charming man my daughter always claimed you were." Just as he was about to offer another excuse, Barbara looked at him and said, "Do it for me."

Luke had no defense to offer against that. Barbara Baxter had been an answer to a prayer for him when he needed someone to be there for Lily, a position he willingly admitted that he couldn't seem to fill, because he had fallen apart himself.

He sighed. "You fight dirty, Barbara Baxter."

The smile on Barbara's lips humored her son-in-law's observation. "I know."

Resigned, he left the kitchen.

When he came out to join his daughter and the woman who worked for him, he heard Lily laughing at something that her newfound friend had just told her. For a second, he felt as if he was intruding and almost turned on his heel to retreat to his office, which he considered a place of refuge.

But then Lily saw him and came running over to

grab his hand. For a tiny thing, he noted that she had a pretty good grip.

"Kayley said she *made* that cake, Daddy. She bakes. She knows how to make doughnuts, too, but she says they're a lot of trouble. That's why she buys those in the bakery. Isn't that amazing, Daddy?" Her blue eyes were wide with wonder. "I never knew anyone who could make doughnuts. Did you?"

Luke pretended—for Lily's sake—to think the matter over before he replied, "No, can't say that I do, Lily."

Kayley attempted to put her ability in proper perspective. "Your daddy knows a lot of important people, Lily. People who save lives and make people's lives better."

But Lily was her father's daughter and not about to give in so easily. "Doughnuts make people's lives better, too," the little girl protested.

Kayley began to laugh as she hugged the child to her. "I do love your simple way of looking at life, Lily. It would be wonderful if everyone else felt that way about doughnuts."

"Then all the cardiologists would have their hands full," Luke speculated drily.

"Good point," she acknowledged.

Luke found the woman's smile was doing unusual things to the state of his stomach, sending it into something resembling a spin cycle. This was new—and it was unsettling.

Seeking shelter in the familiar and the routine, he looked at his daughter. "It's time for bed, Lily."

His usually obedient daughter surprised him by

pouting. "But I want to visit some more," she insisted, looking at Kayley.

Kayley saw the warning look that rose in Luke's eyes. She was quick to defuse the situation and play the peacemaker.

"I tell you what. As long as it's okay with your daddy, why don't I help you get ready for bed and then, once you're all snug under the covers, I'll read you a story. How's that?" she asked, hoping to win over the little girl.

"That's good," Lily agreed, suddenly seeming almost eager to go to bed. And then, almost as an afterthought, she looked at her father and asked him, "Is that okay, Daddy? Can Kayley read me a story? I like hearing a story before I go to sleep, and Grandma's busy in the kitchen."

Kayley understood that to mean that Luke was not the one to read bedtime stories to his daughter. But then, how could he? Until just recently, he hadn't been getting home before his daughter went to bed.

That needed to change, she thought.

Glancing in his direction, she said to Lily, "You know, maybe your daddy would like to read a bedtime story to you."

"No, you go right ahead," Luke told the woman who had somehow managed to burrow herself into his family's life like a determined jackrabbit. He was more than happy to relinquish the position of bedtime-story reader. He knew without being told that he wasn't animated enough to satisfy Lily anyway.

Small fingers had already locked themselves around hers, pulling on Kayley's hand to lead her upstairs to her bedroom.

"I've got lots of storybooks to pick from," Lily told her.

She was so vibrant and sounded so intelligent that Kayley had to keep reminding herself that Lily had turned five years old only recently. She sounded more like a preshrunk adult, Kayley thought, and she found her utterly adorable. Someday she hoped she would have a child just like Lily.

Once in the girl's bedroom, she was ready to help her prepare for bed. But not knowing exactly how independent Lily was, she gave her space and waited to take her cues when they were offered.

Pulling out her nightgown from the bureau drawer, Lily said, "I'll be right back," and took the garment into the bathroom to change.

Very grown up, Kayley thought.

"I'm going to need help with these buttons," Lily called out to her less than three minutes later.

"You got it," Kayley told her. Very gingerly, she opened the bathroom door. Lily was standing there waiting, with her back to the doorway.

Definitely a little grown up.

"Did you scare our guest away already?" Barbara asked as she came out of the kitchen and walked into the living room. Luke was sitting on the sofa, reading the latest copy of a medical magazine. She looked around for Kayley and her granddaughter.

"Nothing short of a zombie apocalypse could scare that woman away—and I have my doubts about that," Luke added.

"Then where is she?" Barbara asked, her hands on her hips.

Luke jerked a thumb up toward the ceiling. "Upstairs, reading to Lily."

Barbara frowned. "Why didn't you go up together?" she asked.

"Because Lily wanted Kayley to read to her," he answered. "It was her choice."

Barbara sighed as she shook her head. "You know, Lucas, you have a great deal to learn about being a father."

Setting his magazine aside, he looked at Barbara. He'd known it was just a matter of time. The woman always spoke her mind, even though it might take a while. "What is that supposed to mean?"

"It means you have a lot to learn about being a father," Barbara repeated. "I think, since Lily took to Kayley so quickly, it might be nice if both you and Kayley take turns reading to her until she falls asleep."

"I think Kayley can handle it." He didn't add that he just assumed the woman was better at it. He'd never been one to read out loud. "She seems to like interacting with Lily."

Barbara arched an eyebrow as she regarded her son-in-law. "What about you?"

He gave Barbara what amounted to a penetrating, scrutinizing stare. Was she trying to set him up with his physician's assistant?

"What about me what?" he asked suspiciously.

"Don't you like reading to your daughter?"

"Oh. That. Sure," he mumbled awkwardly, although the truth of it was, he didn't. It had nothing to do with

Lily but with his own feelings of inadequacy when it came to that.

"Then why aren't you?" Barbara asked. "Why aren't you up there taking turns reading to your daughter?" she asked again. "Or, better yet, you can both read to her, taking turns reading different pages of the same storybook."

He glared at her for a long, long moment. "You know, if I didn't know better, I'd say that you were trying to play matchmaker. But I do know better because I assume that *you* know better, right?" he asked Barbara, his eyes holding hers.

"I'm sure that I have no idea what you're talking about, Lucas. All I know is that there is a little girl upstairs who is starved for some attention from her daddy, so go upstairs and give it to her."

Luke was about to demur, saying something to the effect that he really doubted Lily cared one way or another if he read to her and most likely would prefer having Kayley do the reading.

But then he shrugged and left the room. Arguing with the female of the species had never gotten him anywhere. He saw no point in doing it now.

Chapter Ten

He could hear the sound of Kayley's voice as he drew closer to his daughter's bedroom. The door was open, and as he had expected, Kayley was reading a bedtime story to Lily.

Luke recognized it immediately.

It was the story of a happy-go-lucky little tugboat that never listened. But when a storm at sea threatened to sink a big ship, it was the little tugboat that managed to come through and save the day.

The story obviously pleased Lily, but it also made his daughter think, something that brought a smile to Luke's lips.

"But he was so little," Lily protested. "How could he help?" she asked Kayley.

"It didn't matter that he was little. He had a big heart," Kayley told her. "And most important of all, he wouldn't give up. The big ship needed him or it might sink and the tugboat wasn't about to let that happen."

"I guess he was brave, wasn't he?" Lily asked, clearly impressed by the little tugboat.

"Oh, very brave," Kayley answered with feeling.

Eavesdropping and making sure that neither Kayley nor Lily could see him if they looked toward the doorway, Luke couldn't help wondering how Kayley could sound so enthusiastic about a make-believe character in a children's book.

"Can I hear the story again?" Lily asked in a voice that sounded as if she was growing sleepy.

Luke was certain that Kayley would tell his daughter that once was enough and that it was time for Lily to go to sleep.

Instead, he heard her say, cheerfully, "All right. Now close your eyes," and then she began to read the story all over again from the beginning.

And then a strange thing happened. Rather than walking back downstairs—after all, he wasn't needed—Luke leaned against the doorframe and listened to Kayley read the story about the brave little tugboat.

Again.

She was good with kids, he thought. She'd managed to calm down that young patient of his when the boy was terrified of having an MRI scan done, and Lily had opened up to her in less than an evening. The little girl hadn't opened up to him like that since he'd returned home.

She'd been dealing with her mother's death, but Lily was still dealing with that tonight and yet it didn't seem to interfere any with her warming up to Kayley.

Abruptly, Luke realized that Kayley had come to the end of the story for a second time.

He heard her pause for a moment, then ask, "Would you like me to read it to you again, Lily?"

There was no answer from Lily. Nothing but the sound of her even breathing.

"Guess the second time's the charm," he heard Kayley say to herself. He peered in to see her rising from the side of the bed. Kayley tucked the blanket closer around his sleeping daughter. "Sleep tight, sweetheart," Kayley murmured.

Turning down the light but not turning it off, she slipped out of the room. The second she did, her breath caught.

"How long were you out here?" she asked, startled to find Luke standing just outside his daughter's bedroom.

"You were halfway through the first reading," he admitted.

She felt a little self-conscious. Was there a reason why he'd hung back? "Why didn't you come in?"

Luke shrugged. "You looked like you were getting along very well with Lily and I didn't want to disturb you."

That made no sense to her. "You're Lily's father. You wouldn't be disturbing anything if you came in," she told him.

Not wanting to pursue the subject, he changed it. "Were you really going to read that story to her a third time?" he asked, curious. The story was simplistic and she struck him as an intelligent woman. How could she have the patience to read that story out loud once, much less two and possibly three times?

It didn't seem like a big deal to Kayley. "If she wanted me to, I would have."

Luke shook his head in wonder. "You really do have a lot of patience, don't you?" he marveled.

The only thing she had ever been impatient with was cruelty. Everything else for her was just a matter of going with the flow.

"Well, I have nowhere else I have to be—and to be honest, I've always liked that story." She smiled as a fond memory came back to her. "I can remember my mom reading that to me."

He looked at her incredulously. "Identifying with a kid again?"

The corners of her mouth curved in rather a compelling way. "Something like that."

"Well, I'm sure that Lily appreciated it. I haven't seen her that animated since—" He gave the matter some consideration. "Well, I haven't seen her that animated, period."

Kayley's smile widened. "You have a great little girl there, Doctor."

Hearing her call him that in a personal setting just didn't feel right. Wondering if he was starting a precedent, he still thought that he should change the rules. "I think that in view of the fact that you read that storybook to Lily twice and since we're in my home, you can call me Luke."

Kayley eyed him uncertainly. She already referred to him that way, but only in the confines of her mind. This was taking it to another level completely. "Are you sure?"

"Since I've come home, I haven't been sure of anything outside of the operating room," he told her in a moment of honesty. "But we'll try this out. Unless it makes you uncomfortable," he qualified. His intent was to make her more comfortable, not less.

"No, it doesn't make me uncomfortable," she told him softly. "Does it make you uncomfortable?" she asked, knowing that he was not exactly the most easygoing man she had ever encountered.

"I'll tell you what makes me uncomfortable," he heard himself saying to her even as he wondered where this was coming from. "You make me uncomfortable, but in a way that I can't really put my finger on."

Kayley raised her head, her eyes meeting his. She felt an odd sensation in her stomach. Something akin to butterflies. But she pushed ahead anyway. "Good uncomfortable or bad uncomfortable?"

"There's a good uncomfortable?" he asked, wondering what her definition of that was. He was beginning to think of Kayley as a unique person.

"Yes," she told him, surprised that he had to ask. "Like when you challenge yourself to strive for newer heights. You're not comfortable, because you're forcing yourself to go out of your comfort zone—but you strive for it anyway."

He laughed shortly. "Well, I've got to admit that I'm definitely out of my comfort zone, talking to you like this."

She wouldn't have known it. His expression hadn't changed an iota. "Ah. If you want my opinion, I'd say you're doing rather well."

Luke shifted slightly. He was *really* out of his element now. "Yes, well, I think we'd better go downstairs before Barbara sends out a search party, wondering what happened to us. It doesn't take all that long to read a kid to sleep."

Kayley laughed. "You'd be surprised."

The sound of her laughter seemed to swirl directly into his stomach, and just for an instant, he felt this overwhelming desire come popping up out of left field. The desire to kiss this impossible woman who could so easily remember being a child.

Where the hell had that come from? Luke silently demanded the next moment. Why was he thinking of something like that? He hadn't been with a woman since Jill. And before Jill, everything was just a blur—as it should be.

He was tired and thinking crazy, Luke told himself. Without a word, he led the way downstairs.

Barbara was sitting in the living room, sipping a cup of chai tea. She looked up as they entered the room. "I was beginning to think maybe you got lost," she told them, a hint of a smile playing on her lips.

Luke thought of that fleeting moment he'd just experienced. He'd definitely gotten lost, but he was back now—and he had his bearings.

"Almost," he said, more to himself than to his mother-in-law.

Barbara glanced from her son-in-law to the young woman who had managed to charm her granddaughter. She could sense something was going on and wondered if Luke was even aware of it. She'd loved her daughter dearly and was glad that Jill had loved Luke as much as she had. It was what every mother wished for her daughter, a good, decent man to love who loved her back.

But Jill was gone and Luke needed to find his way back to the living.

Barbara's eyes shifted toward Kayley. "Would you like some chai tea, dear?" she asked.

"No, thank you. It's getting late and I should be getting home," she told the woman. "Thank you for inviting me," Kayley added warmly. "Dinner was wonderful and I loved meeting you and Lily."

"The feeling is mutual." Barbara smiled. Then, thinking of her granddaughter, she said, "She is something special, isn't she? She's five going on thirty," the older woman commented. "Only children tend to be older than their years. They grow up faster than children with siblings."

Kayley could relate to that. "I know. I was an only child. Can't tell you how often I wished for a brother or sister. But Dad died when I was very young and Mom was too busy earning a living and raising me to date anyone. I didn't realize that until I was older," Kayley admitted ruefully.

"I'm sorry to hear that. I have a feeling you would have made a wonderful big sister," Barbara told her, patting her hand.

Kayley felt moved. "You know, I think that's probably one of the nicest things anyone ever said to me." She hugged the woman.

Stepping back, Barbara asked one more time, "Are you sure I can't interest you in some tea?"

But Kayley shook her head. Darting a glance at Luke, she suspected she was close to having overstayed her welcome.

"No, thank you."

Undeterred, Barbara gave it one more try. "Coffee, perhaps?"

Kayley laughed, touched that the woman would try so hard to get her to remain. She would have, but for the sake of her working relationship with Luke, she had to decline.

"I really have to be getting home," she said, glancing in Luke's direction again. She could sense the man's relief at hearing her refusal.

"Well, much as I'd like you to stay a little longer, I certainly can't tie you up and keep you prisoner," Barbara said with a laugh. She eyed her son-in-law. Luke looked like he was ready to sit down again. The man had to be led, Barbara thought. "Lucas, why don't you walk our guest to her car? I'll stay here in case Lily suddenly wakes up."

He couldn't very well protest or say that he'd stay behind while she walked Kayley to her car. That didn't seem right.

"That's okay," Kayley told both of them. "I can find my own way out. It's not like my car is parked in a parking structure or down another street," she said, deliberately giving Luke a way out.

But because she did, it made him feel less than gallant about hanging back the way he actually would have preferred to.

So instead, he said, "No problem. It's dark outside."

Kayley laughed. "It's not like I'll lose my way in ten feet."

Barbara chose that moment to intervene, putting an end to the dispute. "Now, dear, let him feel chivalrous. These days that's usually rather difficult to do.

This might be Lucas's only opportunity to act gallantly for weeks."

"Well, if you put it that way," Kayley said. "I guess that I can't deny letting a man feel chivalrous," she agreed.

Barbara patted her on the shoulder before she sat down again. "That's the spirit." Sitting down, she waved her son-in-law and Kayley out the door.

Without thinking, Luke took her arm, guiding her out the door.

"I'm sorry about that," he said once they were on the front step. He closed the door behind them, making sure that his mother-in-law wasn't listening in.

Kayley's eyes narrowed a little as she tried to understand what he was apologizing for. "Sorry about what?"

Now he knew Kayley was just being polite. "Barbara tends to like to get her own way and she can be a little pushy."

That certainly didn't bother her. Kayley smiled fondly.

"She reminds me a little of my mother," she told him. Then, in case he had any doubt about her meaning, she added, "And that's a good thing."

The path that led down the driveway was well lit, both from the streetlight and from the lights coming from the front of his house.

Just as she was about to turn toward her vehicle, which was parked across the street, Kayley glanced down. And that was when she saw it. There was a bright, shiny new penny right in her path.

Without giving it a second thought, Kayley quickly bent down to pick it up. She'd stopped abruptly without giving Luke any warning, causing him to walk right into her as she stooped over the coin.

The unexpected contact almost caused her to pitch forward and she would have done just that had Luke not grabbed for her, pulling her to her feet and throwing her off balance. Her body hit against his. Air whooshed out of her and she found herself looking right up at him with less than half an inch between them.

Temptation, fast and furious, appeared out of nowhere, taking control while his brain went on temporary hiatus for about ten seconds.

Before he realized what he was doing—and the consequences that would come with it—Luke found himself kissing Kayley.

Lightning shot through his veins, reminding him that he was more than just a skilled surgeon, more than just a walking shell of a man who had trouble relating to the people around him.

It took everything he had not to pull Kayley even closer to him and deepen what was already an electrifying kiss.

She had no idea it was going to happen until it happened.

But once it did, she had to admit that she was exceedingly happy that it had. It was almost as if destiny had taken over—and for this tiny moment in time, it was her destiny to be kissed by a man she both respected and found exceptionally attractive, if not exactly sympathetic.

But sympathy, she knew, was something that could be worked on and developed. However, kisses that were able to shake her down to the very bottom of her feet and up to the roots of her hair were something that could *not* be developed or acquired. They came from something that was either there or not there.

And in the case of Dr. Luke Dolan, it was most definitely there.

So much so that it took her a moment to get her bearings when he drew away. She tried not to breathe as hard as she felt capable of doing.

"I'm sorry," he apologized. "I didn't mean to—"

The rest of his apology was silenced as she put her finger to his lips.

"Don't apologize," she implored.

Whether she said it to absolve him of any guilt or to prevent him from ruining the moment, she didn't say.

Kayley left him wondering about that as she crossed the street, got into her car and pulled away.

He remained in the driveway, staring after her for a very long time.

What the hell had just happened here?

Chapter Eleven

Luke had no idea just what to expect Monday morning. Since Saturday evening, he'd already gone through a dozen scenarios of how his first encounter with Kayley would play out.

In half of them, he would stumble through some sort of an apology about kissing her, saying he had no idea what came over him. In the other half of the scenarios, he would just go on as if nothing had happened between them.

Either way didn't sit well with him.

And then Monday morning came and, one way or another, he had to face the situation.

Just as he was about to leave for work, anticipating yet also dreading getting his first encounter with Kayley over with, Lily called out to him from the top of the stairs.

"Daddy, wait!"

Her hair tousled from her night's sleep, looking as if she'd just gotten out of bed, Lily was still wearing her nightgown. She was clutching an eight-by-ten sheet of paper in her hand and flew down the stairs in her bare feet, obviously determined to get to him before he left.

"Lily, I'm in a hurry," he told her, thinking that whatever she had to say would wait until he got home tonight.

"I know—you're always in a hurry," Lily replied with a touch of adult-like weariness in her voice. "I just want you to give this to Kayley."

"This" was the paper she had brought down with her. She held it up for his benefit. He saw that it wasn't just a piece of paper. It was a drawing that Lily was displaying proudly.

"That's Kayley and me," she told him. "She's reading the storybook about the tugboat to me and I'm in bed, falling asleep."

"That's very nice, Lily," he said, trying to hand the picture back to her. Giving the woman a drawing from his daughter represented far too much intimacy between his physician's assistant and his family. "I'm not sure where she can put it, Lily."

Lily's confidence never wavered. "She'll find a place. Grandma puts the drawings I draw for her on the refrigerator," she reminded her father. "Take it," she urged, attempting to put the paper into his hands.

He didn't want to mislead his daughter, but this was a door he didn't want to open. He certainly didn't want to set a precedent, either. And he didn't want Lily getting any closer to Kayley than she already felt she was.

"Why don't you put it in your briefcase, Lucas?"

Barbara suggested, pulled to the living room by the sound of his discussion with Lily. "That way it won't get bent or wrinkled."

Happy with the idea, Lily stepped over to her grandmother's side and slipped her hand into the older woman's. She smiled up at her, evidently grateful that at least someone understood her.

"Right," Luke murmured under his breath as he snapped open the two locks on his briefcase, laid the drawing right on top of the folders he had there and then closed the lid again.

"Now you'd better get going. You don't want to be late getting in early," Barbara said to him, tongue in cheek.

"I'll see you two tonight," Luke replied, opening the front door and stepping outside.

"Tell Kayley I said hi!" Lily called after him.

Barbara added her voice to her granddaughter's. "Ditto!"

Luke grunted, not really giving either of them a discernible answer.

How had all this gotten so out of hand? Luke wondered as he drove to work. His life was unsettled and complicated enough as he merely came to grips with everything while conducting his practice. He didn't need this extra layer on top of everything.

He found Kayley standing next to the main suite's doors, waiting for him just as she had been the first day she'd interviewed for the position.

Damn, he'd thought that he'd have some time to regroup.

How much time do you need? You already had the

weekend. You're not cramming for your MCATs, he admonished, remembering the tests he'd had to go through when he was applying for medical school. *You're just talking to a woman. The woman who's working for you. Why are you so worried? You're in the driver's seat here, not her.*

Somehow that didn't seem to help make him feel in control.

"Trying to avoid traffic again?" he asked, recalling the excuse she'd initially used to explain why she'd turned up so early.

"The city's doing some repaving," she told him. "I swear we must have the best streets in the country. But since the crews are out, I thought I'd just take a precaution. They tend to block off small sections for hours before they start to work and traffic backs up for blocks."

Kayley waited for him to unlock the doors. When he did so and still hadn't said anything, she had a feeling it was because he was uncomfortable about the kiss they had shared on Saturday. She had to admit that it had been on her mind ever since it happened, but she doubted that Luke thought of it in the same terms that she did.

She sensed that broaching the subject would only make him even more uncomfortable, so she dived into another aspect of the evening she'd shared with his family and him.

"How's Lily?"

He kept his back to her. He thought it was more prudent that way. "Awake."

Kayley laughed. "Well, I would hope so. I've been

known to put people to sleep, but not into a two-day coma."

She was being upbeat. Maybe he was making too much of that kiss.

And then he thought of the drawing in his briefcase. He'd almost made up his mind not to give it to Kayley. Why forge another link in a chain between them that he had no interest in creating? But he had an uneasy feeling that either Lily or his mother-in-law might call Kayley and ask her if she liked the picture that Lily had drawn. He had no desire to be on the receiving end of an inquisition conducted by all two and a half of the women.

"Come to my office," Luke instructed her in what amounted to a gruff voice—at least, that was what it sounded like to Kayley.

Squaring her shoulders, she followed Luke into his office. But the moment they got there, she closed the door.

"Why did you just do that?" he asked, not sure what to anticipate.

He wasn't all that experienced when it came to women. Jill had captured his heart in high school and she had been his only serious girlfriend. Had he insulted Kayley by kissing her Saturday? Was she going to threaten to report him for inappropriate behavior or give him some sort of other ultimatum?

"Because I want to clear the air between us," Kayley answered.

Luke still didn't know if he could believe her. "By saying what?" he asked suspiciously.

"That I had a really great time on Saturday. I think

that your former mother-in-law is a great hostess and your little girl is nothing short of adorable. If I were you, I'd make sure to be home every night to read her bedtime stories."

He waited, but nothing more came. "And that's it?" he asked.

Kayley's eyes met his. "That's it," she replied without a hint of waffling or indecision.

"And what happened—" Luke began, trying to find the right way to mention what had occurred when he walked her to her car.

But Kayley cut him short. "That's it," she repeated firmly, obliquely letting him know that she had no intention of bringing up the kiss they'd shared. It had happened and now it was in the past. End of story.

At least, that was what she assumed he wanted it to be.

Luke was simultaneously relieved and perplexed regarding the same issue. *Why* wasn't Kayley saying anything about the elephant that was very clearly in the room?

The next moment, he told himself to leave well enough alone.

Kayley reached for the doorknob, about to turn it and let herself out of his office.

"Wait a second." Luke put his briefcase on his desk, then snapped opened the locks.

Now what? Kayley wondered, eyeing the briefcase. "You want me to sign a statement to that effect in blood? That there's nothing else?" she guessed.

"No," he answered, then added wryly, "although that might be interesting."

Luke stared down at the drawing lying on top of the folders. He had a strong feeling that he was about to do something that, once done, he couldn't undo. But that was undoubtedly the paranoia talking, he told himself. It was, he had come to realize, a holdover from his time overseas, where every moment was spent worrying that something might suddenly go wrong and life as he knew it would be forever changed.

Except that he had thought it would be because of some injury that he received.

He had received an injury, he reminded himself. It hadn't been a physical one. His injury had been one of the soul. If he hadn't been deployed, if he'd been there with Jill, maybe the car accident would have never happened.

If—

"Doctor, are you all right?" Kayley asked, peering closely at him. "You have a very strange look on your face."

Rousing himself, he told her crisply, "I'm fine."

And then he realized that despite the fact that they were standing in his office with the door closed and were alone for all intents and purposes—definitely out of anyone's earshot—she had called him Doctor. Not Luke, but Doctor. Another concern averted. She wasn't about to be personal at work even after Saturday.

He cleared his throat and told her why he'd brought her into his office.

"Lily stopped me on my way out this morning. She wanted me to give you this." He removed the drawing from his briefcase and handed it to Kayley.

The normally talkative physician's assistant took

the drawing from him without a word. He did hear a small intake of breath, but no other sound emerged from her mouth.

Was she trying to find a polite way of saying that the drawing was very nice when in fact it was a mass of very bold colors and just barely recognizable for what it was supposed to depict?

"She said to tell you that it's the two of you, with you reading her a storybook while she's in bed," he explained.

"I know what it is," Kayley told him in what had to be the smallest voice he had ever heard her use.

And then, when she raised her eyes to his, he understood why she sounded so different. She was crying. At least, he assumed that those were tears shimmering in her eyes.

And then one slid free and slipped down her cheek, so he knew he was right.

"It's not that bad, is it?" he asked, trying to figure out why she was crying.

"Bad?" she echoed, stunned that he would use that word to describe what she was holding in her hands. "This drawing isn't bad—it's beautiful. It has to be one of the most beautiful things that anyone has ever given me."

"Don't get out much, do you?" he quipped before he could stop himself.

"No, actually, I don't," she admitted with a smile he could describe only as shy curving her mouth. "Saturday was the first time I wasn't either working or sitting at home trying to get my mother's things in order since I moved back to Bedford. All the friends I had when I was growing up are scattered and gone," she said in a wistful voice, "and the friends I have now are all up in San Francisco."

"No new friends down here?" Since he'd returned, he'd cut off all ties to everyone except for his mother-in-law, but he had to admit, given Kayley's personality, what she had just said surprised him.

"Not yet," Kayley answered. "Unless you count a certain little blond-haired artist," she added, gazing down at the drawing he'd just handed her. Kayley pressed her lips together and looked up at him. "Thank you for this."

"Not my doing," he told her just in case Kayley thought he had put his daughter up to drawing it. "Lily drew it and she wanted you to have it."

She understood all that. She also understood that he wasn't anxious to promote any extra ties between them. She suspected that kiss had frightened him more than he was willing to let on. Maybe because it made him realize that he could have feelings—in a minor way—for a person other than his late wife.

"But you didn't have to give it to me," she pointed out.

"That would be withholding property that wasn't mine," he replied.

She studied him briefly. She wasn't sure if Luke was being serious or just pulling her leg. "Are you really that honest?"

"To a fault," he confessed.

He *was* being serious. "Honesty is never a fault."

Her comment brought back memories. Luke laughed drily. "Tell that to some of the interns and residents that I ticked off along the way."

She was surprised that he would reveal something like that to her. Maybe they had come a little further along than she'd initially thought. "Really?"

"Really."

She thought for a moment. "Well, there are always two ways to say anything."

"The right way and the wrong way?" he guessed at the standard answer.

But Kayley shook her head. "I was thinking more along the lines of the harsh way and the more thoughtful, delicate way."

Her Pollyanna attitude amused him. "And how would you suggest what the delicate, thoughtful way of saying 'You're the last doctor on earth who should be treating a patient' is?" he challenged.

"Definitely not that way," she answered, then told him, "Doctor, I think for the sake of your daughter *and* your relationship with your daughter, you need a little help in finding a way to let the nicer you finally come out."

She was really barking up the wrong tree. "There is no nicer me."

Kayley was not about to accept that. "At the risk of irritating the 'unnice' you, I beg to differ. I glimpsed the nicer you on Saturday when you were helping your daughter set a 'trap' for a leprechaun. And just now, when you gave me the picture that Lily drew. You could have just as easily left it in your briefcase and I wouldn't have been the wiser, you know."

Luke snapped his fingers. "Damn, I guess I missed my chance."

She smiled then, and again, he noticed that her eyes

seemed to light up each time she did that. The sight fascinated him even though he knew it shouldn't.

"Yes, you did," she told him.

He found himself battling a strong urge to repeat Saturday's mistake.

Chapter Twelve

For a very intense second, Kayley sensed the electricity in the air, the pull between them. But this wasn't the time or the place for it, even if there was no one else in the entire suite of offices.

Kayley had the sensation that she was standing on quicksand and needed to move before it was too late for her to do anything but give in to this attraction—and there would be consequences if she did that.

"I'd better get to work," she told the doctor, trying her best to sound upbeat.

The next moment, she opened the door and made a quick exit from Luke's office.

Luke sank down in the chair behind his desk, staring at the space where Kayley had just been.

He blew out a breath. Maybe he was just over-thinking this, making too much of the whole thing.

Kayley seemed to be unaffected by what had happened between them on Saturday, so he really shouldn't have to worry about it having any adverse effects on their relationship at work. And their relationship at work, he insisted, was all he was worried about, because he didn't have any room in his life for other relationships.

He had all he could handle. He had his surgical practice and he had his daughter. His plate, as the old saying went, was full.

But what about his life? a small voice in his head asked. In the wee hours of the night, when he was alone in his bed, his life felt incredibly empty somehow.

Luke shook his head, as if to shake that thought loose and out of his brain. He was getting carried away, he told himself. He wasn't looking for anyone or anything more than what he had.

And yet...

Less than fifteen minutes later, Kayley burst into his office. "Doctor, you're wanted in the ER. One of your former patients was just brought in by ambulance and he's asking for you."

"I've got a full schedule today," he protested, glancing at the computer monitor on his desk.

"But the ER said he was specifically asking for you," Kayley stressed. She couldn't see how he could just ignore a plea for help like that.

Reluctantly, Luke relented. He supposed that she did have a point. "Call the ER back and ask them the nature of the emergency and who the patient is."

Kayley didn't have to make another call to the ER. She already had all the information he was asking for. "It's a motorcycle accident right along Pacific Coast

Highway. Kyle Brubaker broke his left leg in two places and possibly shattered his knee, as well. He insisted that the ambulance bring him here, to Bedford Memorial Hospital."

"That qualifies as an emergency, all right," Luke agreed. "All right, call them back—tell them we're on our way."

That caught her off guard. Had he just made a mistake? "We?" she questioned.

"Yes, you're coming with me," he told her.

She was convinced she wasn't hearing the doctor correctly. "Excuse me?"

He sighed, stopping for a moment. "You're a physician's assistant, right?"

"Right," she answered, still somewhat mystified as to what was going on. Was he trying to teach her some kind of lesson for butting into his life?

"Well, I'm asking you to come and 'assist' me. What is so confusing about that?" he asked.

Kayley looked at him, stunned. He'd given her no indication that he felt he could rely on her this way. She'd stepped in for the last doctor she'd worked for, but Luke had been rather hard-nosed about things up until now.

"Wouldn't you be better off with another full-fledged surgeon assisting you? Kyle Brubaker sounds like he's going to need surgery on that leg."

"If I wanted another 'full-fledged surgeon' assisting me, I would have told you to stay here." He scrutinized her for a moment. "Your résumé says that you've had surgical training, Are you afraid you won't come through in a pinch?"

It was all the challenge she needed. She had performed procedures more than once for the doctor she had worked for prior to Dolan. "Watch me."

"Oh, I fully intend to," Luke promised.

There were now several administrative assistants at the front desk as they passed it on their way out. Luke paused long enough to leave instructions with the woman sitting closest to him.

"Sheila, reschedule my morning patients. Tell them I was called away to an emergency."

Sheila looked from the doctor to the woman leaving with him. "Yes, Doctor," she murmured.

"We'll be at Bedford Memorial," Kayley added as they were on their way to the elevator.

The receptionist's knowing expression faded just a little.

Pressing for the first floor, he glanced at Kayley. It was an unguarded moment and she looked a little uneasy, in his opinion. "What's the matter?"

She welcomed the opportunity, but she gave him one last chance to change his mind. She didn't want him taking her with him for the wrong reasons and then regretting it. "Are you sure you want to do this?"

"Do what? Play God while I'm putting together some twentysomething's leg because he's a daredevil who takes too many chances?" His shrug told her that he had no choice. "That's what I signed on for."

"No, I meant taking me with you to assist in Brubaker's surgery."

There was almost the barest hint of a smile on his lips. He was daring her. And himself.

"It's time to see what you're made of, Ms. Quartermain. Unless, of course," he said as they got off on the first floor, "the sight of blood makes you feel queasy."

"As long as it's not my own, I can handle it," she replied flippantly. "I just thought you'd want someone at your side who you're used to working with in the OR, that's all."

Luke paused at the street corner directly across from the hospital's emergency entrance and pressed the switch for the crossing light to turn green.

"There's always a first time before there's a 'used to,'" he told her.

The light turned green and they both hurried across the street and entered the hospital's compound. Kayley laughed. "I guess in an odd sort of way, that makes sense," she responded.

"So does that mean you're up for this?" he asked, rather certain of her answer.

"I'm up for this," she replied. Kayley just didn't tell him that her heart had moved up in her throat, where it was probably liable to remain until Dolan's patient was moved to the recovery room.

Her heart did not remain in her throat. It couldn't, because it was racing too hard all during Kyle Brubaker's leg-and-knee reconstructive surgery to stay lodged there. As the surgery progressed and her mettle was challenged, she realized that this was as close to an out-of-body experience as she felt she was ever likely to have. She could almost watch herself competently assisting Luke during the surgery.

When they'd gone in, part of her had assumed that he was just bandying terms around and that he only wanted her to watch him and some other surgeon work on the patient.

But she wasn't just passively watching; she was

right there in the thick of the surgery with him. Being awed by his expertise and by the fact that she could keep up, doing everything that he needed her to do in order to help make the final outcome of the surgery a success. Not for him or for her, but for the patient.

An eternity later, when the operation was finally over, Kayley didn't know that she could feel this wiped out and still be standing upright.

In her opinion, the patient was wheeled out to the recovery room not one second too soon. She felt as if her knees could no longer support her.

She took small, careful steps out of the operating room, then collapsed into the first chair she came across. The chair was one of several lined up along the wall next to the OR and was meant for patients' relatives waiting to hear how the surgery had gone.

From the looks of it, she thought, scanning the area, Kyle Brubaker's parents hadn't been able to get to the hospital yet.

Luke pulled off his surgical mask and took the seat beside hers. To her surprise, he turned his attention to her. "How do you feel?" he asked.

"Like somebody used my body to wipe the decks of the *Titanic*." She shifted to face him. "And yet I feel oddly exhilarated, as well," she confessed.

He laughed quietly under his breath. "Never quite heard it described that way before," he said. "Welcome to the world of orthopedic surgery," he told her in a completely emotionless voice, and then went on to say, "You did good in there."

The compliment caught her utterly off guard. She definitely hadn't been expecting it. "I did?"

He didn't think of her as being capable of false modesty, so her reaction had to be genuine. "Don't look so surprised. I knew you had it in you even if you didn't."

"I'm not surprised that I came through," she told him honestly. "That's what I'm supposed to do." And although he made her somewhat uneasy, she did have a clear understanding of her abilities. "I'm just surprised that you'd tell me I did."

He contemplated her words for a moment. "Am I that much of an ogre?" he asked.

"No, not an ogre," she quickly denied. "You're just that...reserved," she said at last, feeling that she'd found a safe word to describe his particular distant approach.

The slightest of knowing smiles played on his lips. "That wasn't what you wanted to say."

"I always say what I want to say," Kayley assured him, but there was a certain look in her eyes that left him wondering about the complete validity of that statement.

He began to rise. The surgery was over, the patient was in recovery and he had to be getting back. "Well, I've got patients to see," he reminded her.

Kayley sighed. Suddenly, his office seemed miles away instead of just across the street. "That requires walking, doesn't it?"

He slanted a glance at her. "Well, I'm not about to carry you across the street, if that's what you're indirectly hinting at."

"A sense of humor," Kayley acknowledged, staring at him. "Wow. Who knew?"

His expression never changed. "I was being serious," he told her.

Just then, an ashen-faced couple in their mid- to late fifties came hurrying up to the OR.

It was the frantic-looking woman who spoke first, her words tumbling over one another in a nearly garbled fashion. "We're looking for a Dr. Dolan. Our son Kyle was in some kind of motorcycle accident." She pressed her lips together as a sob escaped. The next second, squeezing her husband's hand to the point that his fingers took on a very red hue, she said, "I told him not to get that motorcycle. I *told* him."

"I'm Dr. Dolan," Luke said, interrupting the woman as he reverted back to his extremely formal, reserved persona.

"Is he all right? Is our son going to be all right?" Mrs. Brubaker asked, almost aggressive in her grief as she all but assaulted Luke with the question.

Kayley immediately sensed that the man beside her was searching for words. He might be a total miracle worker in the OR, but when it came to words, his ability to find any that offered even a shred of comfort totally failed him.

Hoping he wouldn't chastise her for this, Kayley came to his rescue. "His left leg was broken in two places and he shattered his left knee," Kayley told the accident victim's parents. She avoided looking in Luke's direction. Even so, she thought talking to the parents was the least she could do for Luke. He had already shown that he had no idea how to go about softening blows or comforting loved ones.

Hearing the description of the injury, Kyle's mother made an unintelligible noise.

Kayley was quick to set the woman—and her husband—at ease. "But the doctor managed to repair the damage, and given time and physical therapy, your son should make a full recovery."

"Well, I know that the first thing he's going to do is sell that damn motorcycle of his," Kyle's mother declared.

"And you are?" Kyle's father asked her, speaking up for the first time.

Kayley waited half a second for the doctor to validate her position. When he didn't, she did it herself. Obviously, he was content letting her do all the talking, she thought.

"I'm Kayley Quartermain. I assisted Dr. Dolan. Your son is in the recovery room right now. After about an hour, they'll be moving him to his room. You can see him then," she told the motorcyclist's parents. "Until then, why don't you go down to the cafeteria while you wait?" she suggested. "They have some really bracing coffee. It might do you some good," she added kindly.

"Thank you," Mr. Brubaker said. "I think we will." He nodded at Kayley and then the doctor she was speaking for.

With that, the couple supported each other as they left, seeming a great deal better for having been able to put some of their immediate fears to rest, at least for the time being.

That fact wasn't lost on Luke.

"You're pretty good when it comes to running interference," he commented.

Kayley shrugged off the compliment as if what she'd done were no big deal, at least not to her. The last thing she wanted was for the doctor to think she wanted to be flattered.

"I thought you looked like you might need to have someone intercede with the guy's parents." She paused briefly, waiting. When he said nothing, she asked, "Did I speak out of turn?"

"No," he answered.

In truth, he had to admit that having her there to talk to Kyle's parents had turned out to be a relief. He'd never gotten the knack of being able to say the right things to patients' loved ones and that included knowing how to reassure them. Words had never been that important to him. It was the deeds that always counted.

"I'm not much of a people person," he stated matter-of-factly.

"Some people just have a harder time than others when it comes to communication," she said philosophically. "But no one could ask for a finer orthopedic surgeon, and when push comes to shove, I'm sure Kyle's parents would have much rather had their son successfully operated on than had a good conversation with you about the procedure." Even as she said the words, she realized that she was paraphrasing something he had told her the first week she'd been hired.

Luke said nothing in response, but he had to acknowledge, at least to himself, that she did have a gift for saying things that put situations into perspective—and that in turn made him feel better.

It wasn't that he felt bad about not being able to communicate, but it was a shortcoming that he wasn't happy about. He didn't like having shortcomings, even minor ones.

"I think you might have missed your calling," he told her as they went to the first-floor locker rooms located behind the OR. They'd both donned surgical scrubs and he was more than ready to get back into his regular clothing.

"I messed up in the OR?" Kayley asked. She'd been confident that she had done well.

"No, you did very well. Surprisingly well," he conceded.

She was confused. "Then why did you just say that I missed my calling?"

Separated from her by a wall of lockers, he quickly changed back into his regular clothes. "Because you could have been on some kind of philosophical debating team, the way you seem to be able to twist and turn words to your advantage."

She guessed that was a compliment, although it could be taken otherwise.

"I'm not as brilliant as you are," Kayley said honestly, briskly shedding her scrubs and slipping back into her own clothing. "That allows me to see things in a more simple light. I don't overthink things. That's why you might have a problem," she said earnestly, adding, "You overthink things. That gets in the way of you being able to relate to everyday average people."

She came around the front of the lockers, carrying her scrubs and looking to deposit them somewhere. "Maybe it would help you if you just think of what you'd want to hear in a similar situation. You know, that old adage—think of yourself as walking a mile in someone else's shoes."

He took the scrubs from her and dumped them, along with his own, into a receptacle. "Well, in the first place, it's not sanitary—"

"Pretend that it is," she coaxed, overriding his complaint. "See, you're overthinking again. Keep it simple," she told him, then smiled. "I guess that's what you have me for."

"Is that why I hired you?" he deadpanned.

She grinned at him. "I'd say it was as good a reason as any."

He laughed softly to himself as they left the locker area. "You just might have something there."

Chapter Thirteen

Without Luke fully realizing it until sometime after the fact, he found himself relying on Kayley more and more in his day-to-day dealings with his patients. Since she had demonstrated her capability during the emergency reconstructive surgery, he had her doing pre-interviews with his patients. He also had her scheduling and reviewing X-rays and scans, as well as administering anti-inflammatory injections to those of his patients he felt could benefit from them rather than surgery. He trusted her to draw conclusions for him to read over and consider before he ever interacted with his patients.

This interdependent relationship was definitely something new for Luke. He was fully aware that he'd never been one to work well with others. Oh, he could work with them but there'd always been a bit of abrasiveness or prickliness involved that interfered with the regular flow of getting things done.

Kayley was different.

She seemed to be amenable to anything he needed while simultaneously subtly interjecting her own take on the situation. The result was an amalgamation of both their inputs to ultimately compose one solid acceptable whole.

He wasn't entirely cognizant of any of this on a conscious level at first. All he really noticed was that things were going well.

Very well.

Consequently, Luke found himself not escaping to work but actually being happy about coming to work each day, which in turn made him a happier man at home. That made him come across in a better light in both spheres.

Both his daughter and Barbara commented on that fact in their own ways, Lily's statement being the more direct one.

"You seem nicer, Daddy," she told him out of the blue at dinner one night.

"Nicer?" Luke asked, pausing to look at the pint-size adult sitting across from him. "What do you mean, nicer?"

She'd blossomed in the last two months, unafraid to speak her mind instead of just remaining silent. "Your eyebrows don't come together so much anymore. You know," she prompted when he didn't seem to understand, "like you're mad at everything."

Luke raised his eyes to look at his mother-in-law, a silent question in them.

"What she said," Barbara told him, pointing toward

her granddaughter and preferring to let Lily speak for both of them.

"I'm not mad at everything," Luke protested, about to say that he never had been and had no idea where Lily had gotten that idea, but he never got the opportunity to continue.

Lily had become a great deal more articulate in the last couple of months. More articulate as well as frank, she went right to the heart of what was on her mind. "Can Kayley come over for dinner again? She hasn't been here in a long, long time and I want to see her again."

He glanced again at his mother-in-law, silently asking if she had put Lily up to this, but Barbara spread her hands wide, disavowing having anything to do with the little girl's request.

"She's direct, like her father," Barbara told him, a hint of a smile curving her lips. She didn't bother attempting to hide it from him.

"Well, Kayley's busy—" Luke began, only to be ambushed.

Lily talked quickly, a lot more quickly than she used to. It left little room for him to offer an objection against anything she said.

"But she'll listen to you. Ask her, Daddy. Please, please, please, ask her to come over. She can't say no to you. You're the boss."

"Wonder where she got that idea from," Barbara remarked under her breath just loudly enough for her son-in-law to hear.

"I can ask her to come to dinner," Luke told his daughter in a tone that said acquiescence wasn't a foregone conclusion. "But she might be busy."

"Busy every night?" Lily asked innocently, as if even she knew that wasn't possible.

Luke wasn't fast enough to suppress the laugh that surfaced. The corners of his mouth turned up as he shook his head. "You've got it all figured out, don't you, Lily?"

Lily didn't answer. She merely continued looking at him with her wide, earnest eyes until he promised to ask Kayley "as soon as you get into work, Daddy."

But Luke didn't get a chance as soon as he got into work.

Since he'd taken to arriving at the clinic at a regular time—except for that Monday morning after Kayley's first dinner with his family—he no longer was the first one there to unlock the main doors to the orthopedic offices. His schedule that day was straining at the seams and he didn't have two minutes to rub together until well after what was supposed to be the lunch break taking place between noon and two.

It was closer to two.

He waited until he was alone in his office and fairly confident that most of the staff as well as the doctors he worked with were still out to lunch, running errands or doing their rounds.

Rather than buzzing for her to come in, he sent Kayley a text.

No sooner had he pressed Send than there was a knock on his door.

That caught him off guard. Maybe there was someone else in the office, he thought. One of the staff had to have come back early. "Come in."

But it wasn't someone else; it was Kayley, responding to his text. Had she been somewhere in the vicinity and he'd missed her?

"You wanted to see me, Doctor?" Kayley asked, popping her head into his office.

He congratulated himself on not reacting to the sound of her voice or the sight of her face. Lately she came across like the first ray of sunshine in the morning and that worried him.

He was afraid that someone else—or perhaps even Kayley—noticed his response. He was trying to keep that all under wraps until it went away on its own.

"Come in and close the door," he instructed, his voice deep and resonant.

She did as he asked.

Since she'd assisted him with that motorcycle-accident patient, she felt that things had been progressing rather well. She'd let her guard down a little, and while still maintaining a respectful air, she had kidded with him in off moments.

Had she inadvertently crossed some line? Did he resent her asking after Lily and his mother-in-law? She was getting personal, but she really did like both the little girl and Barbara and honestly wondered how they were doing.

And, if she was being honest, although most of the time he tried to maintain a distant, blustery air, she liked Luke, as well.

Maybe more than liked him, she amended in the next moment. Was that it? Was that the problem? Had he called her in because he sensed her shift in feelings? Had he caught something in her gaze when she'd assumed he didn't notice the way she was looking at him?

Her mother had always told her to meet everything head-on.

"Did I do something wrong?" she finally asked Luke when he said nothing.

"I'm not sure," Luke replied, slowly picking his way through what he viewed as a verbal minefield. He never took his eyes off her face as he said, "My daughter and her grandmother both asked me to invite you to dinner again, so you be the judge."

Kayley eyed him uncertainly. Her first reaction was to happily accept the invitation, but *was* it an invitation, at least from him—or was it just from Barbara and Lily and he was extending it under duress? She wasn't sure.

"Do *you* want me to come to dinner?"

"What I want doesn't matter," Luke said quite honestly.

Kayley raised her chin in what appeared to be almost a combative manner. "It does to me. I'm very flattered that they'd ask me." Her eyes met his. "But I don't want to come to dinner if you don't want me to be there."

"I never said that," he denied.

"Not in so many words," she agreed. "But there's a look on your face that tells me you're delivering the invitation under protest."

He had a feeling she was being truthful with him. That meant she didn't want to accept if the invitation wasn't from all three of them. But he didn't want to say he wanted her to come, too, because that would be admitting more than he was ready to admit.

So he tried diversion. "Tell me, have you always

had this overactive imagination, or is it something that came over you gradually?"

"I just pick up on signs," she told him simply.

"Obviously, you need to study the language a little better."

"Does that mean you *do* want me to come to dinner?"

"I am a grown man. I don't do what I don't want to do."

"So that's a yes?" Kayley asked brightly.

Luke was nearing the end of his patience. "Are you coming or not?" he asked.

"Coming," she fairly sang back, making her choice, the one she'd made from the first moment he'd told her about the invitation. "Just tell me the day."

"Saturday, of course." He thought since she seemed to have burrowed into his life, she already knew that. "As it so happens, I'm off this weekend."

She smiled and he watched her eyes crinkle, trying not to be drawn in by the sight. "I know. I arranged your schedule, remember?" Her hand on the doorknob, she opened the door, ready to slip out, then added one last thing. "I'll bring dessert."

"You'll bring yourself," he informed her. "Dessert's being taken care of."

"Yes, it is."

He saw the reflection of her smile in the door's glass just as she went into the small hallway.

Why that all-but-see-through image should captivate him, he hadn't a clue.

He had even less of a clue why it should remain with him for the better part of the afternoon.

* * *

When she arrived home that night, Kayley found another penny. It was lying in the gutter, right in front of her mailbox. She'd gone to get her mail right after she'd parked her car in the garage. She'd almost missed seeing the penny, but she'd dropped a letter and when she stooped to pick it up, her fingers had brushed against the copper-colored coin.

She knew it was silly and the height of superstition to believe that the penny had been deliberately placed there rather than that it was just a random occurrence.

Picking up the coin, she folded her fingers over it and held it tightly. She could have sworn she felt a warmth against the palm of her hand.

Kayley smiled to herself for a moment, then whispered, "Hi, Mom. Still watching over me, I see."

Kayley took the rest of her mail out of the box. From the looks of it, there were a few random ads, an appeal for a charitable contribution and two bills, along with her weekly copy of a popular magazine. She tucked all of it under her arm.

"Made any new friends, Mom?" she asked as if she were carrying on a conversation with her mother the way she used to. She walked to her front door. "I've been trying to move forward just like you told me." She unlocked the door and turned on the light even though it was still daylight outside. And then, unable to keep the words bottled up inside any longer, she said, "I met someone, Mom."

Kayley walked over to the side table against the wall and put her mail there. She also deposited the penny she'd picked up and placed it in a small ceramic bowl where she put all the pennies she found.

Lately she'd found more than she thought was her share, which was why part of her was certain that her mother was watching over her. It wasn't anything that she would admit to anyone else, except for possibly her godmother.

Maizie, she knew, believed in things like that, just as she did.

"But I guess you already know that," she went on with a smile. "He's a doctor and I think he needs me, Mom. Not like a doctor needs a physician's assistant," she hurried to explain, as if her mother were standing right there, listening. "He needs me to help him get over the hurt he's feeling. His name is Luke and he lost his wife. I think he also lost his way. There's a little girl involved. Lily, his daughter. You would have loved her, Mom. He was having trouble relating to her, but I hit it right off with her. In a way, that opened the door for him to relate to her. Or at least, to start to. All in all, I think that's going along pretty well."

She sighed, gazing off into space. "I miss you, Mom," she whispered, feeling her eyes sting a little. "You would have made everything right right away."

"She's here! She's here!" Lily called out. The little girl had been keeping vigil at the living room window that faced the driveway for what clearly seemed like forever to her. "Daddy, she's here!"

"I heard you, Lily," he answered, walking in from the dining room. "I think that the whole block probably heard you." He saw Lily throwing open the front door. Belatedly, he realized what she was doing. "Lily, don't run out!" he called after her, but it was too late.

Lily had dashed out of the house to greet her new

best friend, forgetting all the rules that she'd been given.

Luke ran out after her, envisioning the little girl darting out in front of the car before Kayley had a chance to bring her vehicle to a full stop. Possible consequences haunted him.

His heart was in his throat as he got to the driveway. "Lily!"

Standing in the middle of the driveway, his daughter looked over her shoulder and gave him what had to qualify as one of the world's most innocent looks.

"Yes, Daddy?"

He'd reached her side by the time Kayley got out of her car. Her eyes swept over the beaming little girl and the ashen-faced doctor, two very opposite ends of the spectrum.

"Is something wrong?" Kayley asked, sensing she had just walked in on something possibly volatile.

"Yes, something's wrong," Luke retorted, struggling not to show just how much his daughter had frightened him. "Lily ran out of the house the moment she saw your car pulling up. She knows that she's not supposed to do that." He turned toward his daughter. "What if that wasn't Ms. Quartermain?" he demanded, barely able to restrain his anger.

"But it was," Lily replied, obviously bewildered by her father's reaction.

Kayley decided to step in and referee before things really escalated.

"What your daddy is saying is that lots of cars look alike and you need to make sure you really know who the person is before running out to meet them. Also, it's a good idea to wait until the car that's approaching comes to a full stop. Sometimes brakes don't work as well as they should. You can wait a few extra seconds. Your daddy loves you and he doesn't want anything happening to you," Kayley explained.

It was evident that Lily was doing her best to digest everything that was being told to her. A completely contrite-looking little girl turned her face up to her father.

"I'm sorry, Daddy," she told him. "I didn't know I was making you worry."

The wind totally taken out of his sails, Luke had no recourse but to place his arm around his daughter and accept her apology.

"That's all right, Lily. Just make sure that doesn't happen again," he said.

"I won't," she promised solemnly. "The next time Kayley comes over, I'll wait until she knocks on the door before coming out." She punctuated her statement with a beatific smile. Then, looking back at her idol, she asked, "Is that okay, Kayley?"

"That's perfect," Kayley said, and kissed the top of her head.

Kayley beamed, completely unaware of the fact that her words had just launched Lily's father into a total quandary.

Lily had said "the next time," which meant that she fully expected to have her idol come by more often, possibly on a regular basis.

Just what had he gotten himself into, Luke couldn't help wondering.

And why wasn't he more upset about it?

Chapter Fourteen

"So are we all meeting out here in front of the house instead of inside again?" Barbara asked, referring to the first time Kayley had come over to dinner. "Why didn't someone tell me?" she quipped, coming out to join the others on the front step.

And then she smiled at Kayley. "Hello, dear, so nice to see you again." Glancing at her son-in-law, Barbara went on to add, "It's been much too long," as she embraced the younger woman.

A familiar scent swirled around her when they made contact. When Barbara released her, Kayley commented, "I like your perfume."

Barbara smiled fondly. "Thank you. My husband first gave it to me on what was to be our last anniversary. It became a favorite of mine."

"My mother used to wear that same perfume," Kayley told her.

Barbara nodded with approval. "Your mother had good taste."

"Can we move this along?" Luke urged. Without thinking, he placed an arm around each of the two women's shoulders, ushering them toward the opened front door. "I'd really rather not stand out here where the neighbors can hear everything we say,"

"He's a very private man," Barbara pretended to whisper to Kayley.

Kayley suppressed a laugh as she responded in a stage whisper, "Yes, I know."

Luke wasn't amused. "Inside, ladies," he said forcefully. "We'll talk about me inside."

Both women laughed in response, as if they were sharing a joke. Not to be left out, Lily joined in even though Luke was fairly sure his daughter had no idea what was going on or why her grandmother and Kayley were laughing.

The whole scene, intimate in nature, had a familiar feel.

Almost *too* familiar, he warned himself.

He was going to have to be careful that he didn't complacently slip into an overall accepting mode of behavior. Yes, he was growing more comfortable again with Barbara and Lily—which was good—but he had to remember that Kayley was *not* part of the family unit. She was just a woman who got along well with his mother-in-law and his daughter, nothing more.

He *had* to remember that, Luke silently repeated.

"I brought you something," Kayley told Lily just before they walked into the dining room to eat dinner.

Lily looked all around Kayley before she finally said, "Are you teasing me? I don't see anything."

"That's because it's little," Kayley told her. She took a shining gold-foil box out of her purse and handed it to Lily.

Excited, Lily opened the box and found a small gold pendant inside.

"It's a leprechaun," Kayley told her. "At least, it's a leprechaun charm. I thought you might like to have it until you finally catch a real leprechaun with your dad."

Lily's eyes were shining. "I love it!" she declared. "Put it on me," she begged, directing the plea to Kayley rather than to her father.

"Okay," Kayley told her. "Now lift your hair up and hold still."

The moment the clasp was closed, Lily ran to the mirror hanging over the sofa in the living room and inspected her appearance.

"It's beautiful," she cried. "Isn't it beautiful, Daddy?" she asked, showing it off to him.

"Beautiful," he agreed.

He looked on as Lily threw her arms around Kayley and hugged her to show her appreciation.

The display of his daughter's unabashed joy got to him. He tried his best not to appear moved, but it wasn't easy.

Despite his unspoken warnings to himself, dinner turned out to be filled with laughter, shared stories and an overall good feeling. He completely forgot to be on his guard and wound up just enjoying the evening. Between the laughter and the company, Luke felt like a different man. Or, more accurately, he felt like the man he used to be. The man who had existed before tragedy had gutted him, removing his heart and just about everything else that Jill had loved about him.

Everything that had made him human.

Luke chalked up his transformation—temporary at best—to the way Barbara and Lily were acting, lighthearted and happy. But if he was being honest with himself, he knew it wasn't just them—it was him.

And it was Kayley.

After dinner, and partially against his will, Luke found himself recruited to play not one but two different board games with all three women. He grumbled for form's sake, but that, too, had a comforting, familiar feel to it, and just for the evening, he decided to go with it.

Lily's bedtime seemed to arrive all too soon, even though he'd allowed the exact time to be moved back by half an hour. Twice.

Finally, he had to remain firm so that his daughter didn't think of him as a pushover. Forcing himself not to look down into the pouting little face, he announced, "Lily, it's way past your bedtime. Time to put the game away."

Lily sighed, knowing there was no more bargaining over this point.

"Can Kayley read me a bedtime story?" Lily asked hopefully.

Kayley felt her heart being tugged. But she didn't want to trespass any further into Luke's territory than she already had, and glancing at him, she could see that he actually wanted to read to his daughter.

"I think maybe your daddy would like to read to you, honey," Kayley tactfully pointed out.

He was about to demur, yielding the task to her, when Lily came up with her own solution. "Both of you can read to me. You can take turns."

Kayley laughed. The child was a natural peacemaker. "Well, that's an offer I certainly can't refuse," she told Lily, then looked up at Luke. "How about you?"

"Please, Daddy?" Lily pleaded, turning her electric-blue eyes on him.

"How can you say no to those eyes?" Kayley asked her boss.

A joint venture. His back was against the wall. Luke knew he couldn't turn his daughter down without coming across like an ogre. "I can't."

Kayley affectionately ruffled Lily's silky hair. "Looks like you have yourself two storybook readers tonight, Lily."

"Yay!" The little girl grabbed them each by the hand and tugged them in the direction of the staircase and her room, just beyond the landing. "Let's go," she declared.

Luke found that it took a while to settle his daughter down. Once she had changed into her pajamas, brushed her teeth and crawled into bed, pulling up the covers, he and Kayley took turns reading to Lily, each taking a page—the suggestion had been Kayley's.

He was fairly certain that Lily preferred it when Kayley read to her because Kayley sounded far livelier than he did. For one thing, the woman did different voices and intonations when she read, while he could only be himself and read the story in his own voice.

It felt like it took a while, but eventually, when he was reading to her, Lily finally fell asleep. Pausing, he watched the sweet face, expecting to see some sign that she was struggling to stay awake.

But her eyelids remained closed.

With a sigh, Luke closed the book that he was reading, nodding to himself. "Always knew I could put her to sleep."

Kayley raised her eyes to his. "She was tired," she pointed out in a hushed voice.

"You don't need to sugarcoat it," he told her, setting the book aside. "I'm perfectly aware that I sound monotone and boring. I can't do cute voices the way you do."

She frowned. That was a cop-out and he knew it. "*Anyone* can do cute voices," she informed him, rising to her feet. She paused to pull the covers up around the little girl. They'd slipped down slightly. "You just have to get out of your own way and not be so self-conscious. Let the inner you out."

She crossed to the bedroom door, then waited for him to join her. Very quietly, they slipped out and eased the door closed behind them, leaving a night-light on for the little girl.

"I can teach you how to do it," she volunteered as she went down the stairs first.

But Luke shook his head, turning her down. "That's all right," he told her. "I'm perfectly happy being boring."

She stopped at the bottom of the landing. There was that word again. "Boring?" she repeated incredulously. "You are not boring," she insisted with feeling. "You just have to have enough faith in yourself to let that inner you loose."

There was that term again. He didn't know what this woman thought she knew about him, but she didn't.

"The 'inner me' doesn't know any funny voices, either," he said. "And he doesn't want to 'let loose.' 'He' is just fine the way he is," Luke informed her.

For a moment they stood there, silently regarding one another, entertaining thoughts and feelings that at least one of them knew were way out of line and should be stifled.

Kayley could feel her pulse beginning to accelerate, could feel herself growing just a wee bit warmer. She was afraid that if she acted on what she was feeling, there was a very strong possibility that she wouldn't be able to find her way back.

And worse, she just might frighten Luke off and lose any small ground she might have gained. Moreover, if things went badly and Luke wound up distancing himself from her, she wouldn't be invited back. If that happened, she would really miss seeing Lily—and Barbara, too, she silently added. The woman *did* remind her a great deal of her mother, and although she *knew* Barbara wasn't her mother, she had to admit that it was nice to have that faint sliver of a memory drifting through her head.

"I understand totally," she finally answered Luke, doing her best to sound cheerful. *Time to go home, Kay*, she told herself. "Well, I had a lovely time but I should be going home," she said out loud.

She walked away from Luke, then paused by the living room and peered in. "Thank you for the wonderful meal, Barbara—and best of all, for the company," she added.

"Are you leaving already?" Barbara asked, looking upset. "Can't you stay a little longer?"

"No, I really think that I should be getting home," Kayley told the older woman with a smile. She turned toward Luke before saying, "Thank you both for everything."

Kayley picking her purse up from the side table where she'd deposited it and made her way to the front door. Without a backward glance, she opened it and let herself out. She did not realize that Luke was right behind her until she reached her car and unlocked the driver-side door.

It took effort not to gasp when she saw a hand reaching around her to open the door for her. Swinging around, she saw Luke standing as close to her as a shadow.

"Oh, you startled me."

"Sorry, I thought you had eyes in back of your head," he quipped.

"They're not standard-issue for physician's assistants," she told him, recovering. Her heart, though, took a few seconds to return to its natural rhythm. "That doesn't happen unless we become full-fledged physicians—or mothers," she added fondly.

For the most part, the evening had gone very well. But now she thought she detected a hint of tension coming from Luke. Maybe he didn't like feeling obligated to see her off. Most likely, he wanted to be back in the house.

She tossed her purse onto the passenger seat, then told Luke, "You really don't need to do this."

"Do what?"

She gestured toward her vehicle. "Walk me to my car."

He blew out a breath. Whether it was from exasperation or not, she had no idea. "As I recall, we had this conversation last time."

Kayley did her best to remain upbeat. "Still just as valid."

"If I didn't come out with you," he pointed out, "Barbara would think I was some kind of a boor." Remembering what he'd said about boring his daughter to sleep, he specified, "The kind with no manners, not the kind that puts people to sleep."

He couldn't believe that, Kayley thought. "I really doubt she'd think anything of the kind. Barbara seems to know you very well—and she holds you in high regard from what I can tell."

He glanced toward the house. "Yes, I lucked out as far as mothers-in-law go. She's a very good woman," he said gratefully. "Another woman might have held her daughter's death against me."

Kayley was convinced that had to be a slip on his part. He wouldn't have willingly allowed something so personal to just come out like that. For a second, she thought of saying something noncommittal and dropping the subject.

But that just wasn't in her nature.

"You had nothing to do with her daughter's death," she told him firmly.

He felt differently about that. "If I were here at the time, I would have been the one in the driver's seat, not Jill. And the other car would have hit me instead of her," he added emotionally.

With the wealth of information available on the internet, she'd done some research regarding the collision that had claimed his wife's life. "The accident happened on a weekday in the middle of the day, didn't it?" she asked, knowing it had.

"Yes, but that didn't have anything to do with it," he insisted.

"I don't mean to argue with you, but it had everything to do with it. You would have been either in the office or at the hospital at the time, busy being a doctor. And as awful as it sounds, your wife still would have been in the driver's seat." Compassion filled her eyes. "You have to stop beating yourself up for your wife's death," she told him quietly. "It was not your fault. Barbara doesn't blame you. Anyone can see that. It's about time *you* stopped blaming you," she said forcefully.

Luke felt something crack inside.

Torn, he didn't trust his reaction just then, didn't trust himself to not say something he would regret tomorrow morning. He needed to regroup, to rethink things before he did or said anything.

For now, Luke stepped back as he allowed her to slip into the driver's seat. "I'll see you Monday."

"Monday," she repeated with a nod, a small smile on her lips.

At least he hadn't fired her for being outspoken, Kayley thought. Some would call that progress, she congratulated herself as she drove away.

"So?" Barbara asked her son-in-law the instant he walked back into the house.

"So?" he repeated, puzzled.

Barbara sighed. The man was a brilliant surgeon, but when it came to the business of living, not so much. "So did you ask her out?"

He stared at the woman as if that had come out of nowhere. "Why would you think I'd ask her out?"

"Oh, Lucas, Lucas, Lucas," Barbara lamented, shaking her head. "Perfect strangers passing by your house can hear the chemistry that's crackling between the two of you."

"There is no such thing as perfect strangers," he informed his mother-in-law. "And I have no idea what you're talking about."

"Don't you?" Barbara questioned, studying him closely. When he made no response, she threw her hands up in exasperation. "Life, Lucas. I am talking about life."

"What about life?" he asked, daring her to continue along this line.

But he had forgotten just how strong willed his mother-in-law could be. And she wasn't backing off.

"Get back in it, Lucas, before you completely forget how to do that. That young woman cares about you—you can see it in her eyes. More than that, she cares about Lily. And Lily needs a mother."

Luke felt himself growing defensive. This was Jill's mother. How could she be trying to pair him off with another woman? Didn't she have any allegiance to her daughter or to the past?

"Lily has you," he pointed out.

Barbara shook her head. "I am her *grand*mother, Lucas. There's a difference." She put her hands on Luke's shoulders to keep him from walking away the way she could see that he wanted to. "My daughter fell in love with a dynamic young doctor who was willing to grab life with both hands—to save lives and live life."

He sighed. It felt as if his mother-in-law were talking about an entirely different person. Someone he *used* to be. "That died with Jill."

"But it shouldn't have," Barbara argued. "Lucas, I appreciate you grieving for my daughter, I do, but she would have wanted you to move on, to be the man she fell in love with—and to find happiness. You owe it to her, Lucas. You owe it to Lily, and most of all, you owe it to yourself."

He inclined his head, knowing that arguing was a lost cause when it came to his mother-in-law. So he took the easy way out and told Barbara, "Okay, I'll think about it."

"Do more than just 'think' about it," Barbara pleaded. "People like Kayley don't come around often and they don't linger indefinitely. Ask her out before someone else does," she advised. "You have nothing to lose—although you will if you don't ask her out," she predicted.

"Like I said," he told her as he started to go up the stairs, "I'll think about it."

Barbara sighed. "Lucas," she called after him, "I love you like a son. Think fast," she counseled. "Please."

Luke just continued walking up the stairs.

Chapter Fifteen

"That was really a nice thing you did," Luke said the following Monday morning as he walked into the small room that Kayley used as an office.

In the middle of updating and preparing Luke's morning schedule for him—his regular scheduler, Justin, had called in sick this morning—Kayley looked up from her desk, slightly confused. She didn't detect any sarcasm in his voice, so she assumed he was on the level.

"I'm sorry, I'm not fishing for a compliment— really—but you're going to have to be a little more specific than that," she told Luke, having no idea what he was referring to.

He supposed he had started in the middle of his thought. Regrouping, he said, "The leprechaun charm that you gave Lily. She hasn't taken it off since you put it on her. I told her it would last longer if she took it off at night, but she just won't part with it."

"There's no reason it shouldn't last, on or off her neck." And then she realized what he was really concerned about. "If you're worried that it'll turn her neck green or get discolored itself, it won't," she said. "The charm is fourteen-karat gold."

He looked at her incredulously. "Gold?" Luke repeated, stunned. "Why would you buy Lily a gold charm? She's only five."

"A girl is never too young for good jewelry," she quipped. "Besides, I was shopping in the department store when I happened to see it and I immediately thought of seeing Lily and you setting up that trap so she could 'catch' a leprechaun and give it to me as a gift. It really made me happy to be able to give her the charm as a token of our first meeting."

"Well, I can assure you that it made her happy to get the charm." He wanted to frown reprovingly, but he just couldn't make himself do it. "But you really shouldn't have."

"That's your opinion," she conceded, and it was clear that it definitely wasn't hers. "But I felt it was the least I could do since she was trying to catch that leprechaun to give to me as a present."

It amazed him how quickly his physician's assistant and his daughter had taken to each other. "She won't stop talking about you."

The corners of Kayley's generous mouth crinkled in a fond smile. "Good. I might need a publicity agent someday." She looked down at the notes she had made that needed to be input into the computer. "Especially if I don't get this organized for you, because then I might have to be in the market for a new job."

"Well then, I'd better leave you to your work," Luke told her, withdrawing from the cubbyhole of an office and shutting the door behind him.

Luke might have left her presence, but Kayley vividly lingered with him in his mind.

The more he attempted not to think about Kayley, the more he found himself doing just that. Without being "in his face," she had absolutely burrowed right into his head. So much so that thoughts of her would randomly pop up in his mind all day long, whether or not he actually saw Kayley.

Moreover, what also kept preying on his mind was Barbara urging him to ask Kayley out. Not just to a family dinner, but to an actual evening out.

A date.

The idea distracted him all that day and the following day, as well.

The day after, he finally surrendered.

It happened right after one of the orthopedic group associates, a spinal surgeon by the name of Jacob Larson, bumped into him between their offices and asked if he was considering attending Bedford Memorial's annual fund-raiser.

The question had come out of the blue and Luke had no pat answer prepared, so the truth came out in small dribbles.

"I hadn't thought about it," he admitted to Larson. Since the other surgeon was looking at him, Luke heard himself asking, "Should I?"

"Oh, absolutely," Larson said with enthusiasm. "It's always good to show up at one of these things, at least for a couple of hours. The board takes it as a sign that you're really interested in being part of the medical community."

"I thought I did that by being a surgeon," Luke said drolly.

"Man—or woman—does not live by surgical tools alone," the young doctor replied. "Get with the program, man. Operating is only part of what we do. Turning up at one of these fund-raisers builds goodwill all around. You never know when you might need some of that sent your way," he reminded Luke.

Other than going home, he had his evenings free. Luke shrugged, thinking, *What the hell?* "I guess I can put in a showing for a couple of hours."

"That's the spirit," Jacob declared with approval. He started to walk away, then doubled back to add, "Oh, and don't forget to bring someone."

This was a wrinkle that Luke hadn't considered. "I have to bring someone?"

Larson stared at him as if he were talking to someone who was extremely simpleminded. "Well, sure. You don't want to come across as antisocial, do you?"

Being called that had never bothered him. But illogic did. "I'm turning up at a fund-raiser. Doesn't that automatically mean I'm not antisocial?"

"*Nothing* is automatic," Larson assured him. "Besides, a good-looking guy like you should have no trouble finding someone to take to this function."

That wasn't the point or the problem. "I didn't say I'd have any trouble finding someone," Luke began, a little irritated at the suggestion.

Larson immediately cut him off. "Then what's the problem?" he asked.

The problem was that securing a date just might be opening himself up to things that were undoubtedly better left alone.

Luke felt himself warming as thoughts of Kayley surfaced. He quickly shut them down.

Oh hell, this was going to be in a public place, for heaven's sakes. What could be safer than a hospital fund-raiser in a hotel ballroom? And if he asked her out, maybe he'd prove to himself that he was making himself crazy for no reason.

"No problem," he told Larson briskly as he walked away from the spinal surgeon.

"Doctor, are you all right?" Kayley asked when she saw Luke walk by her on his way to his office. He had a strange expression on his face and he looked right past her.

The sound of her voice caused him to come to an abrupt stop. He hadn't even seen her there. He did now. Doing his best not to sound self-conscious, he said, "Yes, why?"

"Well, to be honest, you look like you're contemplating having a root canal done." Even as she spoke to him, she saw that he was now making an effort to appear as if everything were all right. The man was *not* a very convincing actor. "You don't have a patient for another half hour. Maybe you should take a break in your office and try thinking of some happy thoughts to relieve your stress before he gets here," she suggested.

Instead of agreeing—or disagreeing, which she felt would have been more in keeping with his personality— he completely stunned her by asking, "Kayley, would you like to go to the hospital fund-raiser at the Bedford Plaza Hotel this Saturday?"

Kayley looked at him uncertainly, not sure exactly what he was asking her to do. "You mean to represent the orthopedic group?"

It was his turn to be puzzled. Why would she think that he wanted her to represent the entire orthopedic medical group?

"No," he told her, "I mean with me."

Her smile was wide and radiant, like someone who had stumbled across a Fourth of July celebration complete with fireworks totally by accident. "Well, if you put it that way, I'd love to. Will it just be the two of us?"

Again, her question caught him off guard. "And a ballroom full of doctors and their guests."

Kayley shook her head. "No, I meant will Barbara and Lily be coming with us?"

He supposed he could see why she'd think that. Their last two get-togethers had been for dinner at his house with both his mother-in-law and his daughter in attendance.

"Barbara won't be attending," he told her, "And as for Lily, I think they have a minimum height requirement for attendees. Does that make a difference?" he asked. Maybe she felt uneasy without the two females present.

Kayley shook her head. "No, I just wanted to know if they'd be coming along with you." She'd almost said *us* but she had a feeling that would have been far too intimate sounding a word for Luke. "Do you want me to meet you at the fund-raiser, or—"

"No, I'll pick you up," he said, cutting her off.

"Like a date?" she asked innocently, wanting to get everything perfectly clear.

"Like a fund-raiser," he responded almost automatically.

He wasn't comfortable enough to call it a date yet. Maybe by the time the evening arrived, he would be, but for now, he opted to keep the whole idea of a date at arm's length.

"Then I had better give you my address," she told him, taking out a piece of paper so she could write it down.

"That would be helpful, yes," he agreed, catching her hand to keep her from writing. "Why don't you give it to me on Friday?" he told her. "There's less likelihood that I'll lose it that way."

"Understood," she replied, trying not to grin from ear to ear.

Kayley was well aware that this was just an official function tonight. Undoubtedly something Luke felt obligated to attend—or maybe he was even told by one of his peers that he needed to make an appearance. Going to a function solo was uncomfortable and, she felt, left him open to being approached by women who would have welcomed spending an evening—and its aftermath—in the company of a good-looking doctor. In all likelihood, Luke saw her as his shield, someone who could run interference for him for the duration of the evening so that he could concentrate on whatever it was that he wanted to concentrate on at the event.

It didn't matter why he was taking her, Kayley thought. What mattered was that he *was* taking her, she told herself cheerfully, going through her closet and searching for something that seemed special enough to wear to the fund-raiser.

Whatever the reason, Luke had asked *her* to attend the function with him. Her, not someone else. That meant that for several hours, she was going to be next to him and there wasn't going to be any blood, any operating room or any surgical tools involved.

Just a whole bunch of other people, all dressed in their finest.

Any way she assessed the situation, it was a good deal.

Now all she had to do was find something to wear that wasn't going to make him regret asking her to attend.

And then Kayley smiled to herself.

She knew just what filled the bill. It was a dark blue sequined long gown that was simple and tasteful, and once on, it hugged her body like an old loving friend. The gown came with a long slit along the left side for ease of movement as well as ease on the eye of the beholder.

She'd bought the dress on a whim almost a year ago. The sale was just too good for her to resist. She had purchased it telling herself that this was her "someday" gown, a gown she promised herself that she would wear "someday," and apparently, "someday" had come—a lot sooner than she'd actually anticipated.

Now all she needed to complete the look, she thought, assessing the gown, were matching shoes and a purse.

Less than an hour of shopping that Friday allowed Kayley to accomplish her mission.

* * *

Anticipation raced through her veins Saturday evening. Wanting to get everything right, she'd been dressed and ready for at least an hour. She was just touching up her makeup when she heard the doorbell ring.

Kayley felt her stomach suddenly pulling itself into a hard knot.

She looked into the mirror. Would Luke like what he saw once she opened the door? Or would he think he'd made a mistake asking her?

"You're going to have fun," she told her reflection, nervously smoothing down her dress. "You haven't been out since forever and it's time that you enjoyed yourself. If Luke likes your gown, great, but this evening's not about what you're wearing. It's about having a good time. Understand?" she all but ordered the woman peering back at her in the mirror.

The doorbell rang again, almost making her jump.

"Coming!" she called out.

Here goes nothing, Kayley thought.

She hurried to the front door and didn't bother pausing to catch her breath before she opened it.

"Hi," Kayley declared brightly, smiling up at the handsome man in the black tuxedo standing on her doorstep.

Luke said nothing for a moment. Words had suddenly become unavailable. The woman he was looking at on the other side of the doorsill all but completely took his breath away.

Her medium-blond hair was "carelessly" piled up on her head in a manner he recalled someone had once referred to as "flirty." The long-sleeved floor-length navy gown she had on shimmered and sparkled, effectively drawing his attention to every single curve she had—and she definitely had just the right number of them.

He'd been aware that Kayley had a good figure, but the word *spectacular* had never been involved before. It was now.

In capital letters.

"Kayley?" Her name came out like a hesitant question.

"Yes," she responded. Seeing the rather stunned expression on Luke's face, she asked him, "Is something wrong?"

"What?" he mumbled, preoccupied with absorbing the vision that was standing in front of him. Then, coming to, Luke played back her question and murmured, "Oh, no, no, nothing's wrong. I just never realized before that the lab coat you wear in the office actually hid that much of you."

"Is that good or bad?" she asked, not certain where he was going with this. Was he telling her that he thought she was heavy? Or did he find that the gown was too revealing?

"Good," he told her, then realized that she might take that as a criticism. "I mean bad." But that didn't sound as if it had come out right, either. "I mean—"

Luke decided he had no recourse but to take both feet out of his mouth and begin over again. "What I mean to say is that you look very nice tonight."

"I'll take answer number three, please," she told him, the corners of her lips curving with pleasure. "Thank you."

Luke made what amounted to an unintelligible noise that sounded like a half grunt.

This was as close to tongue-tied as he could ever remember being since before he reached puberty.

Given his field of expertise, the female form wasn't exactly a mystery to him. He had no idea why seeing Kayley in her formfitting gown would render him a blithering idiot who had suddenly lost the use of his brain as well as his ability to form even simple sentences.

"If you don't like this, I could change into something else," she offered.

"Don't you dare!" The words had slipped out before he could stop them. Realizing how they must have sounded, Luke immediately cleared his throat and tried to backtrack. "I mean—"

Laughing, Kayley came to his rescue. "I know what you mean," she told him without acting coy or fishing for some sort of a compliment. "And thank you." She reached for her white shawl that she'd draped on the back of a chair, handed it to him, then presented her back to him. "Would you mind?"

"I don't think it'll look good on me," Luke deadpanned.

Her smile over her shoulder utterly warmed every square inch of him as she said, "No, I mean helping me put it on."

He nodded. "I know what you mean."

Luke slipped the fringed shawl on her shoulders, and for some reason, even that slightest of contact telegraphed a very strong bolt of electricity between them.

He knew that at least he felt it.

Maybe Barbara hadn't been all that far off in her

comment about there being electricity between them, Luke thought.

The next moment, he shut the thought as well as his reaction to Kayley down and murmured, "Let's go. I don't want to be late."

She spared him a kind, understanding look before going out the door first. "Neither do I," she assured him.

Chapter Sixteen

Kayley had to admit that she felt a little like Cinderella walking into the ball.

Other than on the pages of a fashion magazine, she couldn't recall ever seeing so many beautifully dressed women gathered together in one place before. The men were all well dressed, as well, but the women were in a category all their own.

Definitely Cinderella, she thought.

Entering the main ballroom where the fund-raiser was being held, Luke noticed the way Kayley was looking at the other women in the room, as well as the expression on her face. He'd grown accustomed to seeing a smile there, not this somber look.

"Something wrong?" he asked.

She hadn't realized that she was being that transparent.

"I feel a little underdressed," Kayley answered honestly. "If you're embarrassed to be seen with me, I understand. I'll just slip off into the crowd," she offered.

Luke looked at her as if she'd lost her mind. "Embarrassed?" he echoed. His eyes slid over her from head to toe as if to check that his initial impression had been correct. It was. "What are you talking about? You look perfect."

He said it with such feeling he left her utterly speechless.

But only for a second. Regaining her ability to speak, she decided Luke was only being kind—he'd come a long way in a short time.

"But all these women, they're dressed in such gorgeous gowns—" she protested.

"It's not clothes that make the man—or the woman," he reminded her. "Besides, with most of these women, it's a competition as to who has the more exclusive designer and who is wearing the more expensive gown," Luke told her matter-of-factly. And then his voice lowered. "You never struck me as being that shallow."

"I'm not," she began, but again, she wasn't able to get any further.

"Well then, case closed," he told her. "No reason to discuss it any longer—or to waste time thinking that you don't measure up just because you don't have a year's salary to blow on a dress you can't wear very often. By the way," he said, thinking that perhaps he needed to say something to reinforce her self-esteem, "if I didn't mention it before, you do look exceptionally attractive in that dress."

He had used the word *nice* when he'd picked her up earlier. But this had taken the compliment up to a whole new level. Given that Luke wasn't the type to offer empty platitudes, his admiration meant a great deal to her and warmed her heart.

"No," Kayley murmured, struggling not to let the deep red color she felt rising inside her stamp itself on her face, "you didn't mention it." Her eyes met his. "Thank you."

Kayley was fairly glowing, Luke observed. It seemed somehow intimate to have that sort of an effect on a woman by giving her what he considered to be a factual compliment. It made Luke feel far less removed from her and perhaps even just a little protective toward Kayley.

Don't make too much of this, Luke, he warned himself gruffly.

"Just making an honest observation," he told Kayley. But it was hard to stay gruff, looking at her looking like that. "If Lily had seen you in that, she would have said that her magic leprechaun had turned you into a fairy princess." Hearing himself, he cleared his throat, somewhat embarrassed for saying what he'd just said. "Or words to that effect," he added, vainly attempting to cover up what he saw as his error.

He noticed that Kayley was beaming again.

"They're lovely words," she told him with genuine emotion.

He shifted his gaze away from her and pretended to scan the tables in the ballroom. "Why don't we see where they have us seated?" he suggested.

"You're calling the shots tonight," she told him amicably.

It was just a phrase, he told himself, but for a second, it felt as if she were giving him carte blanche and it started him thinking about what he might want to do if it were truly a case of "anything goes."

Luke found himself entertaining thoughts he had honestly believed he would never think again.

Never feel again.

The next moment, Luke forced himself to mentally retreat from where he had gone. He was here to put in an appearance, not to have fantasies about a woman he was finding himself more and more attracted to. Attracted to both her mind and her skills—and now, he realized, to her, as well.

Clearing his throat again—as if that might in some way help him to clear his mind—Luke placed his hand against the small of her back and guided her over to where he vaguely assumed their place cards were set.

He saw that he and Kayley had been seated at a large table with the rest of the orthopedic specialists. No one had taken their seats yet. They were early.

"Looks like they're going to have us mingling before feeding us," he commented.

Kayley smiled. "I don't mind. I like mingling."

Luke inclined his head. "Then I'll follow your lead," he told her, then confessed, "I don't much care for mingling."

She was well aware of that, which was why his invitation to come here with him had been such a surprise. "We don't have to stay here long," she told Luke. "Just long enough for some of the people on the hospital board to see you. And then we can go."

"You'd be satisfied with that?" he asked.

"I'm satisfied now," she told Luke with a smile. "I got to play dress-up and received a few very nice compliments in the bargain." She looked at him pointedly. "I'm good."

"You certainly are," he heard himself saying. The next moment, Luke attempted to backpedal, just in case Kayley misunderstood what he was trying to convey. "I mean—"

Kayley placed her hand over his in a gesture of camaraderie.

"I understand," she told him. "You don't need to explain. I'm not about to read anything into that," she assured him.

Again, the room was fairly crowded with people, yet he couldn't help thinking that it felt as if they were sharing an intimate moment.

"Would you care for a drink?" a slender young uniformed server asked, intruding into the moment as he held up a tray filled with glasses of sparkling champagne.

Time to regroup. "I certainly would," Luke told the server, plucking two glasses from the tray and offering one to Kayley. When the server withdrew, Luke asked, "Should we toast anything?"

Kayley thought for a second, then said, "How about our work?"

It was definitely not what he'd been expecting. "You're certainly an unusual young woman," he told her. Raising his glass slightly, Luke said, "To orthopedic surgery."

"That needs a little work," she told him. "To *successful* orthopedic surgery," Kayley amended.

Luke suppressed a laugh. Laughter had made a comeback in his life lately, it occurred to him.

"I stand corrected," Luke said just before he took a sip from his glass.

He saw her smile behind her glass and felt something hot and demanding springing up in his gut, stirring it. It was a sensation he hadn't experienced in a long time.

Feeling it now exhilarated him as much as it worried him.

After that, for the rest of the evening, he stayed clear of the champagne, afraid that the alcohol might have simply intensified what he was feeling. He didn't want to take any chances.

Kayley was surprised that they stayed at the fundraiser as long as they did.

She'd thought, once she'd mentioned that they could leave at any time, that Luke would take her up on that, if not quickly, then at least within the hour.

But he hadn't.

They were not the last ones to leave, but they were in the last third. This was after a three-course meal that turned out to be, surprisingly, quite good and then sitting through the fund-raiser. The latter was centered around bidding for a wide variety of prizes that had been donated to the cause by local businesses. The prizes included, among other things, family packages of tickets and added perks to several of the amusement parks in Southern California, three-day stays on the *Queen Mary 2* and trips to Catalina Island.

When a family package to Disneyland that was near and dear to her heart came up for bid, she surprised Luke by getting caught up in the bidding. She was even more animated than usual, going out of her way to top each new bid made on the tickets.

The bidding was heated for several minutes, until it came down to just two bidders. And finally, Kayley outlasted the other opponent, who gave up and dropped out. The family package was hers.

"You do realize that you wound up paying more than the tickets actually cost, right?" Luke asked her after the dust had settled. He was about to point out that she could have easily gone to the amusement-park box office and paid less than what she'd just bid, but he didn't get the opportunity.

"You can't put a price tag on having one of the princesses as your personal guide through the park," Kayley told him after she had written out a check payable to the hospital and collected her prize.

"You're actually saying that with a straight face," he marveled, shaking his head.

"That's because I'm serious," she told Luke. "Here." She held the envelope with the tickets out to him. When Luke didn't make a move to take it, she grabbed his hand and placed the envelope into it, saying, "Lily is going to love this."

The full implication of what Kayley had just done hit him. "You did this for Lily?"

"Well, everyone is young at heart in that place," she quipped, "but yes, I did it for Lily—and for you," Kayley added.

"But why?" He could have easily afforded to get tickets for himself and his daughter—if it had occurred to him.

It was as if she could read his mind, he thought when she said, "Because Lily needs some time with her daddy, and where better to spend that time than in a place where magic happens on a regular basis?"

Kayley could see that she was running up against some resistance on his part, so she tried again.

"She's the little girl who came up with the plan to catch a leprechaun, but you're the one who went along with it, so I think there's just enough of the little boy in you to enjoy this 'magical kingdom,' as well."

"I see." He opened the envelope, confirming what he already knew to be the case. "There're four tickets in here."

"That means you can take Barbara with you. That way you won't get completely overwhelmed by Lily." She grinned. "You'll take turns."

The one who would really not be overwhelmed by Lily was the woman he was looking at. Kayley struck him as having more stamina than any three people he knew.

"Would you be willing to come along?" he asked her.

Willing? She would *love* to, but she wasn't one to presume anything. Kayley wanted to be very, very sure Luke was saying what she thought he was saying. "Are you asking me to come?"

He didn't see where the confusion came from. "They're your tickets."

"No," she corrected him, "they're yours. Or rather, they're Lily's." Because Lily was the person she had done all that bidding for in the first place.

"Well then, there's no need for any further discussion," Luke concluded. "Lily would rather have you come along than me and we have enough tickets for all four of us."

Kayley looked at him, upset. He couldn't possibly believe that.

"That's not true," she insisted. "The only reason she reacts to me the way she does is because I can get down to her level more easily." Her eyes shone as she teased, "But you're getting there, Leprechaun Catcher."

"I don't know why we're going around and around about this, Kayley," he said honestly. "Unless you don't want to go."

She didn't want him misunderstanding—nor did she want to miss out on going. She was just trying to get him to understand how important he was to Lily.

"Of course I want to go," she assured him. "I could never resist going back to that wonderful amusement park. They had a lot less princesses the last time I went. I have to admit that it would be fun to see how things have changed there—but still stayed the same."

"The magic of childhood," Luke declared. And then he looked at Kayley, pleased at the ultimate outcome. "Lily's going to be thrilled," he predicted.

That made two of them, Kayley thought. And then she looked at her watch. "It's almost midnight," she realized. She looked at the envelope she'd won.

"I guess it's way too late to give those tickets to her tonight."

He hadn't realized that it had gotten this late. And that he'd had this much fun being here—but that was on Kayley, he thought. And her "magic."

"I guess we need to get you home before you turn into a pumpkin," he told her.

Kayley looked at him, clearly impressed. "You remember your *Cinderella*," she cried. "I would have never thought that of you." A smile split her face. "Looks like I'm not the only one full of surprises."

"Some things stay with you," he said as if to shrug off any undue credit for recalling anything about a fairy tale.

The lights of the houses in the development where Kayley lived were dark when they drove by them.

"Looks like everyone turns in early around here," Luke commented.

"Well, it is after midnight," Kayley reminded him as they pulled up to her driveway.

He countered her reminder with one of his own. "But it's a Saturday night."

"The people who are taking advantage of that fact," Kayley said as she turned the passenger-side door handle and got out of the car, "aren't home. They're out partying or at the movies."

"You have a point," he agreed. He began to follow her to her front door.

Kayley looked over her shoulder and stopped walking for a moment. "If you want to go home, it's okay. You don't have to walk me to my door and wait for me to open it. This is a very quiet, safe neighborhood," she said.

He pretended to give her a scrutinizing look. "Are you trying to get rid of me?"

"Oh no, quite the opposite." Embarrassed, she turned away and unlocked her door. "I mean, if you'd like to come in for a nightcap, I've got a little beer and some wine in the refrigerator," she offered, remembering she'd pushed both bottles to the rear of the fridge. "I don't really care for either," she admitted.

"Then why do you have them?" he asked.

"Full disclosure, my mom used to have company over. Her friends enjoyed both the wine and the beer—as did she. I like mixed drinks, myself," she told him as they walked into the house. She flipped on the light switch before closing the door.

"So why don't you have that?" he asked her.

"Because the idea of drinking alone is so sad," she confessed.

"You don't entertain?" He knew he was probing, but he found himself really curious about what she did outside the office.

Kayley smiled at the question. "I'm too busy working to do any entertaining."

"You're serious?" he asked her uncertainly.

"Why would I lie about something like that?" she responded. She looked up at him. "Tonight is the first time I've been out in a long, long time."

He believed her. "Then I'm glad I asked you to come with me."

"So am I," she admitted.

Her words were hardly louder than a whisper. He was standing so close to her she was certain she could hear her heart pounding in her chest.

And the next moment, she was certain he could not only hear it but feel it, as well, because he was holding her close as he kissed her and there wasn't enough space to fit an eyelash between them.

Chapter Seventeen

Just an instant later, Luke drew back from her. It was the last thing in the world that he wanted to do, but he wasn't about to allow his emotions and urges to dictate his actions. Most of all, he didn't want Kayley to feel that she had to kiss him.

"Sorry," he said.

"For what?" Kayley asked. "For being human? For allowing *me* to feel human?"

"No, for my presuming too much," Luke replied honestly.

She realized he was being serious. They didn't make Boys Scouts like him anymore. "If you have anything to apologize for, maybe it's for presuming too little," she told him.

It had been years since he'd been in this sort of a situation. Luke felt as if he were inching along, trying to find his way—blindfolded—in completely un-charted terrain.

"Then you didn't mind?" he asked.

Kayley pressed her lips together for a second as she tried to gather her thoughts. It was clear that Luke was going to make her spell this out. Not because he wanted his ego stroked, but because he honestly didn't know how attracted she was to him.

She smiled up at him. "You're not going to leave me any dignity, are you?"

His eyebrows drew together. If anything, he was more confused, not less. "I thought that was what I was trying to do."

"By having me make all the first moves?" she asked in disbelief.

He shifted closer again, his blood heating as he tried to understand exactly what was going on here. "Then you didn't mind my doing this?" he asked, slowly brushing his lips against first one side of her neck and then the other.

With every movement, every kiss, Kayley could feel the anticipation in her veins increasing by what felt like geometric leaps and bounds.

"Last chance," she heard Luke breathe.

Now it was her turn to be confused. "You're leaving?"

"No," he told her, his voice thick with desire. "Last chance to have me stop."

"Oh." Now it made sense to her. "That train has long since left the station," she said, beginning to thread her arms around his neck.

Still wavering, he caught Kayley's hands in his,

holding them steady. "I don't want to do something you're going to regret."

How did she get him to understand?

"The only regret I'll have is if you decide to stop right now and walk away."

Part of him felt that he *should* walk away for so many reasons, not the least of which was that if he went through with this, he'd feel guilty about turning his back on the memory of his wife. But the pull he felt was just too strong to ignore.

"I don't think I can," he told her honestly.

"Good," Kayley whispered just before she rose up on her toes, wove her arms around his neck and kissed him with all the bottled-up feelings that had been threatening to explode within her.

After that, there was no turning back for either of them.

The only path left open was the one that led them forward, to a totally new plateau in their relationship.

His desires unleashed, Luke kissed her over and over again, grazing his lips over her forehead, her eyes, her cheeks and then back to her mouth again.

He kissed her chin, the tender areas of her neck and throat before moving down to the swell of her breasts.

Wanting to feel him against her skin, Kayley urgently undid the zipper at the back of her gown so that in a single heartbeat, nothing remained between his lips and her skin.

Her act of silent surrender increased his need for this woman tenfold and he anointed every part of her with his mouth, his tongue, nipping sensitive parts of her skin with his teeth.

Hearing her ragged sigh added more fuel to the fire, which already felt as if it were burning at top capacity.

Luke undid the hook at the back of her strapless bra. Then with his hands resting on either side of her hips, he gently coaxed the flimsiest of bikini panties down until they floated to the floor around her ankles.

When she drew back from him, Luke looked at her, startled. Had he misread the signs coming from her after all?

And then she smiled wickedly.

"You're overdressed," she told him.

The next second, she was tugging his jacket off his shoulders and down his arms. She repeated the action with his shirt after first unbuttoning it, her fingers moving so urgently she all but tore the buttons off before she managed to push them through the holes.

Undressing Luke was both fast and slow because neither of them could keep their lips away from one another for long while Kayley was stripping away his garments.

She pulled on his belt so hard that she almost ripped the hole that the metal tongue was in. When she finally managed to successfully unbuckle his belt, she went to work on freeing Luke from his last remaining garment. One button undone, one zipper pulled down, and his gray slacks went the way of her gown, overlapping and pooling with it on the floor.

Moments after that, there was nothing left between them but the hunger all but devouring both of them.

Unable to hold back long enough to go up to her bedroom, they remained where they were, allowing the bright flame of their lust to consume them in the living room.

Sinking onto the sofa, their bodies melded into one another, sealed by heat and urgency as they kissed over and over again, leaving no parts of each other's bodies untouched.

Kayley thought she knew what she was in for, thought that there were no surprises for her when it came to lovemaking.

She was wrong.

Luke was both gentle and passionate at the same time, causing desire to crescendo and peak within her not once but several times until she was on the edge of exhaustion.

Just when Kayley thought she was approaching the final moment, the ultimate union, Luke moved her back and began to explore her body all over again, doing so with such thorough movements that he was bringing her to the verge of a climax a moment before it came crashing over her body.

Stunned, she arched up against him, against his wondrous lips and tongue, which had swept her into this uncharted region so effectively. His lips pulled back into a smile against her skin just as an almost guttural sound escaped her.

Her body shuddered as the final effects of the magic he'd performed replayed themselves before they finally ebbed away.

Panting, she found the strength from somewhere to reverse their positions as well as their roles. She wouldn't have been able to do it if she hadn't managed to catch him off guard the way she had.

Feeling utterly brazen and wicked, she began to do to him what he had done to her, stroking him with her tongue until he was all but primed and aching to release.

At the last possible second, he caught her by her shoulders and drew her up along his body until their eyes met. Hers reflected confusion. "Don't you want me to do that?"

"Yes," he uttered almost hoarsely.

"Then why…?" She didn't understand why he'd pulled her up like that.

"The only thing I want more," Luke told her, "is to be able to see your face when that moment happens and the only way for that is for you to be right where you are this moment."

Before she could say another word, Luke wrapped his arms around her and, in one movement, flipped them over so that he was the one who was on top again.

"Traditional?" she questioned, referring to their positions.

"Just this first time," Luke answered with a smile she couldn't quite pin down.

Was he telling her that there would be more times in their future? she wondered, her blood racing again as her heart sang.

His eyes were on hers as he finally brought them together, entering her with barely restrained urgency. Kayley wrapped her legs around him as he began to move within her, starting slowly, the tempo growing with every press of his hips.

Not to be left behind, Kayley mimicked his movements, thrusting harder each time that he did. In the end, it was impossible for her to determine which of them was leading and who was following. They were going on that most intimate of journeys together, urging one another on until they reached the end at once, absorbing the earth-shattering explosion, their bodies and lips sealed to one another's, holding on tightly so as not to be jarred from the face of the earth.

She clung to him on the way down, savoring the aftereffects while she held on to the euphoria, at the same time realizing that it would fade all too soon.

When it did, she felt him slump against her and then disengage their union, moving to her side. Kayley was surprised that he didn't make any attempt to draw into himself, as well. Instead, Luke gathered her to him and pressed a small, precise kiss to the side of her temple.

"Is that your way of saying I did good?" she asked Luke. It would have been teasing if she'd had the energy for that.

"That's my way of saying that you completely wore me out," he told her. Luke exhaled a long sigh, then asked her, "Am I sitting up yet? I need to sit up so I can leave."

She barely contained the laugh that bubbled up in response to his comical question. "I hate to break it to you, but you're still lying down."

"Oh," he said as it that was news to him.

Right now he was being so adorable she was convinced she was in love with him. "Why don't you try later?" she suggested.

"You mean stay here on this sofa like this until later?" he asked as if they were having a serious conversation.

By now she was grinning from ear to ear, delighted that he could be playful like this. "Yes."

"And what will you do?" he asked, continuing the pretense.

"Stay here with you," she answered innocently.

"That's your plan?" he asked, doing his best to sound somber.

Luke could feel her smiling against his side. "That's my plan," she replied.

He pretended to think over what she had just told him. "Can't say there's much to it."

"Doesn't have to be," she answered, lightly and playfully sliding her hand along his chest. "Just has to work."

"Uh-huh." He felt Kayley laughing beside him. Shifting so that he could look at her, Luke asked, "What's so funny?"

Her eyes crinkled slightly as she grinned. "I would have never thought, not in a million years, that you had this in you."

"You mean lovemaking?" he asked, feeding her a straight line.

She waved his words away. "No, that I knew. I'm talking about being so laid-back and actually having a sense of humor."

"You take that back," Luke deadpanned. "I don't have a sense of humor."

That only made her laugh more. "Sorry, too late. Cat's out of the bag, I'm afraid."

Luke's eyes glided over her. She was beautiful, he thought. He realized that he was completely and totally smitten with her, as well as extremely turned on.

"Why don't we see about trying to put the cat *back* in that bag?" he said wickedly.

When he shifted his body completely toward hers, she could feel him wanting her all over again. The man had incredible resilience, she thought. Who would have ever thought...?

Her own thoughts evaporated as he pulled her to him and began to kiss her over and over again. It was hard for Kayley to think of anything except how much she wanted Luke to make love with her again.

Her blood surging, Kayley returned his kisses with ardor, absorbing everything and glorying in the fact that when they'd finished making love the first time, Luke hadn't just abruptly gotten dressed and left. He'd remained beside her, making her feel as if this first time had been special for both of them.

She knew what to expect but was still blown away by Luke's tenderness as well as his passion. Moreover, she knew he was putting her needs ahead of his own without a single word to that effect.

When they'd finished enjoying one another for a second time, Kayley was certain that her heart was just going to explode in her chest. It was hammering so very hard.

And the best part was the way Luke held her after it was over. As if she was precious—and as if he wasn't sorry for the way things had played out.

She'd been braced for that, for some show of regret on Luke's part. But so far, there wasn't any.

Mentally, she crossed her fingers, praying that there never would be. Most of all, she prayed that she was right in believing that this was not the last time they would come together.

Luke knew he should be going home. If Barbara was still awake, she would undoubtedly be wondering where he was.

No, she wouldn't be, he amended. Knowing Barbara, she'd know exactly where he was. One way or another, she had been urging him to make this happen, to move on with his life. You'd think, he reflected, that the woman were *his* mother rather than Jill's.

Even so, he really needed to get dressed and go home… he told himself. In a minute, he hedged. Or maybe five. He just needed to close his eyes for a second and then he'd be up to leaving, Luke thought.

Just another second…

Chapter Eighteen

"Really?" Lily squealed, covering her small rosebud mouth with her hands as she tried to contain her joy.

For his part, Luke had *never* seen his daughter this excited before. Granted, she had been becoming progressively more and more enthusiastic, but this was a new high.

Lily was reacting to the news that a trip to the happiest place on earth was in her near future. He had made the announcement when they'd walked in the door the following morning. He did it in part to distract his daughter from the fact that he was still wearing the same clothes he'd had on the night before.

Kayley had urged him to be the one to tell Lily about the amusement park even though she'd been the one who had scored the family-pack tickets. She hadn't said it in so many words but he knew that she felt he needed to get closer to his daughter by appearing to be the hero in her eyes. Nothing was more heroic to a five-year-old than being taken to the most famous amusement park in the world.

He smiled at her. "Really," he answered Lily.

"And you'll come, too?" Lily asked, grabbing his hand with both of hers as if that would somehow make him agree. Lily might be five, he thought, but it was a wise five. His daughter took nothing for granted.

"I'll come, too," he promised.

On a winning streak, Lily asked him, "Can Grandma come?"

"Wouldn't think of going without her," he told his daughter. Looking over her head, his eyes met his mother-in-law's and he saw the approval on her face. Obviously, he'd said the right thing. Never mind that it was also the truth.

"How about Kayley?" Lily asked, suddenly turning shy on him. It didn't stop her from asking, but she wasn't quite as animated about it now. "Can Kayley come with us? It'll be fun with her," she begged.

He did what he could to keep a straight face. "Meaning it won't be fun with just me?"

"It'll be funner," Lily said diplomatically, if not grammatically. "Grandma likes her, too, don't you, Grandma?" She turned toward her grandmother and asked as if that would seal the discussion.

"Absolutely," Barbara said with feeling, looking over at the young woman she'd been championing from the very first moment she had become aware of her.

"This is a family pack of tickets," Kayley told the little girl. "That means that it's for the family."

Lily didn't hesitate for a moment. "But you can be

part of the family." She looked at her grandmother for backup. "Can't she, Grandma?"

"That would be up to Kayley," Barbara told her granddaughter. "But if my vote counts," she added warmly, "I vote yes."

Lily turned toward her father, raising her hand as far as she could.

"I vote yes, too!" She looked hopefully at him with her wide, wide blue eyes. "Vote yes, Daddy." It was half a request, half a plea.

This was really putting Luke on the spot, Kayley thought. Yes, they'd spent a really wonderful night together, but that was behind them and she didn't want him to think she was one of those clingy women who never let go once she'd gotten hold of a man, no matter how slender that hold was.

She stooped down to Lily's level. "I appreciate you voting for me, Lily, I really do. But I think your daddy wants to spend some fun time with you and your Grandma." She'd come along today to see Lily's reaction when she found out about the tickets and to soak in a little more of the warmth that was part of Luke's family. But now, she told herself, it was time to retreat. "I'll be going now," she said, making her way to the door.

"I drove you here," he reminded her.

Caught up in the moment, Kayley had forgotten that. "I can call a cab or an Uber," she told him.

"Now you're just trying to hurt my feelings," he replied, circling around Lily and coming up to her.

"Your feelings?" she echoed. She had no idea what he was talking about.

"Yes. You're leaving before I had a chance to vote,"

he said. After pausing for a moment to let his words sink in, he went on to say, "I vote yes."

Lily immediately began to jump up and down, clapping her hands together. "That means it's uni-muss," she exclaimed.

If Kayley's smile had been any larger, it'd have been in danger of cracking her face, Luke thought, totally captivated. He was also trying not to laugh at his daughter.

"You mean *unanimous*," he said to her.

"Yeah, that word," Lily agreed without missing a beat. She swung around to look up at Kayley. "You have to come, Kayley. Say you'll come," she insisted, taking her hand and holding it the same way she had done with her father.

Kayley gave it one more try. "And there's no little friend you'd want to go with you instead of me?" she asked.

"You're not so little," Lily agreed, "but you're my best friend and there's nobody else I want to go with us to that happy place. Please?" she said again.

"I guess then it's settled," Kayley said. In case there was any doubt of what she was saying, she told Lily, "Yes, I'd love to go with you."

Again, Lily cheered, this time with such zeal Kayley knew there was no backtracking from the agreement, even if she'd wanted to. Which she didn't.

"By the way," Luke told his daughter and his mother-in-law, "it was Kayley who got the family pack for us. So technically, we are her guests, not the other way around."

Lily threw her arms around Kayley, managing only

to get up as high as Kayley's hips. She hugged the woman for all she was worth.

And then, abruptly, Lily spoke up. "You need to marry Kayley, Daddy, so we can keep her forever and ever and she won't go away." She turned to look at her father to see how he received her suggestion. She didn't notice that her suggestion had caused her idol to turn a really bright shade of red.

"It certainly is something to think about," Luke told his daughter in a bemused voice.

"We can vote on it," Lily responded, excited and fresh off her victory.

It was Luke's mother-in-law who stepped in this time. "This isn't something we can vote on, Lily," she told the little girl gently. "This is something for your daddy and Kayley to decide."

Resigned, Lily nodded, and then glanced hopefully over toward her father. "Can I tell you how I'd vote if I could vote?" she asked.

He laughed, kissing the top of Lily's head. "I think I know how you'd vote," he told his daughter.

Lily looked at him wide eyed. "You kissed the top of my head, Daddy. You never kiss the top of my head. Kayley does that."

His eyes locked with Kayley's. "Maybe I'm picking up her habits," he said.

"How about some brunch?" Barbara suggested, tactfully intruding on the moment. "I'm in the mood to do some cooking. Anyone up for doing some eating?"

"Me!" Lily cried, raising her hand and waving it.

"Looks like the 'mes' carry it," Luke said fondly, taking his daughter's hand.

Smiling up at him, Lily reached for Kayley's hand, as well, before they all headed to the kitchen.

It wasn't lost on Luke, not the way he felt, not the way his daughter reacted. All of this was made possible because of Kayley. She'd opened his eyes, making him realize the way he'd held back from connecting with his daughter, as well as the way he had withdrawn from life.

There was no doubt about it. With her sometimes-annoying optimism and irritating ways of doing things, she'd made him a better father, a better doctor and, in general, a better man.

A man who was taking small, halting steps back to rejoining life.

He kept it to himself for a while, but with each passing day, Luke was more and more certain that he was right. He was a changed man, a *happier* man, because of Kayley.

And he needed to tell her so.

He chose his moment when they were alone.

"You're staring at me," Kayley said one evening as they lay in her bed after they had made love—something that was happening with more and more frequency, much to her happiness. Because it was so special to her, she was afraid that it was going to end, but until it did, she planned to enjoy every single second of it. "Are you trying to find a way to tell me something?"

He was toying with the ends of her hair, just as he'd done before. "Yes."

The second he'd answered her, Kayley's heart shot

into her throat and not in a good way. She could feel it throbbing there.

"I take it it's not that you've decided to postpone that amusement-park trip. Lily is really looking forward to it," she added, wanting to focus his attention on that.

"No, the trip is still on for next Friday," Luke said.

"Would you like me to give up my ticket to someone else?" she guessed. Maybe he was trying to find a way to ask her because he wanted to bring along someone else in her place.

"No."

"You're going to say something more serious, then," Kayley guessed, doing her best not to panic or lose her grip on her emotions.

"Yes."

This was bad, Kayley thought. Luke was responding in monosyllables, the way he used to when they first began working together. And then it hit her. He was trying to find a way to tell her that it was over between them. That whatever they'd had had run its course but Lily was getting too attached to her and he just couldn't stand by any longer and allow that to happen.

Kayley's hands turned icy. She didn't want to force this discussion. If she was being honest with herself, all she wanted to do was run from it. But if she did, it was going to hang over her head the entire time until they had it out.

She might as well face up to what she knew was about to happen.

"I'll make it easy for you," she told Luke.

"That's a first," he couldn't help commenting. No matter how he looked at it, there was nothing "easy" about the woman he'd found himself in love with.

Kayley took a deep breath and then said, "I'll resign at the end of the week."

Her announcement caught him completely off guard. "Wait, what?" Luke cried, stunned. He stared at her in disbelief. "You're quitting?"

"That's what *resign* usually means." Each word felt as if it were burning on her tongue as she uttered it.

Had he missed something? He tried to make sense of what she'd just told him. "Aren't you happy at the office?"

How could he even ask that? She'd done nothing but grin since she'd entered the place. "I'm supremely happy there."

He went through reasons why she would leave. "Did you get a better offer?"

Kayley smiled at him sadly. It took everything she had not to just curl up against him, seeking shelter. But that would only prolong the inevitable. "There is no better offer."

Okay, he gave up. "Then why are you leaving?"

Why was he making her spell it out for him? "Because you want me to."

He stared at her, as close to dumbfounded as he'd ever been.

"Unless we've slipped into an alternate universe, no. Where did you get such a ridiculous idea?" Luke asked.

"I just thought— I mean, I felt—" Kayley was absolutely tongue-tied. Words were simply not coming out the way she wanted them to. "Then you don't want me to leave?"

"Hell, no," he declared, then told her with a straight face, "You're the best physician's assistant I've ever had."

She assumed he was being serious as well as honest. "But you want me to keep out of your private life," she guessed.

"You really are batting zero tonight, aren't you?" he laughed. And then he pulled her closer to him, taking comfort from the way the heat of their bodies blended. "Look, I might have wanted you to stay away at one point, but if you did that now, I'd feel as if my life was caving in." He gently caressed her cheek. "I went through that once. I barely made it out alive. I don't think I'm up to handling that again. In fact, I know I'm not."

Kayley felt a tiny spark of hope begin to flutter its wings within her chest. "Then you don't want me to leave?"

"No," he told her emphatically, "I don't."

Relief flooded through her veins so quickly it almost made her dizzy. She wanted to throw her arms around him and hug and kiss him until the end of time, but she held back until she could get him to answer one question. "But when I turned toward you, you looked like you wanted to say something to me."

"I did. I do." Why was this so hard? "Something serious."

Kayley braced herself, though now that she knew he wasn't going to ask her to leave, she thought she could weather anything. "What was it?"

"I want to ask you if you would consider—not now, but someday when you're ready," he qualified nervously "—if you would consider marrying me."

Maybe her heart was hammering too hard and she'd misheard him. "What?" she cried.

He tried again, but he felt his nerve ebbing. He'd

faced down armed militants in Afghanistan, but a slip of a thing, naked to boot, made him break out in a cold nervous sweat.

"Like I said, not now, but someday when you're ready," he qualified again. "It's just that you've made me want to live again, Kayley. With that cheery commando approach of yours, you've made me happy and, quite honestly, I can't imagine life without you. And neither, I know, can Lily. So if—"

Kayley stopped him by putting her fingers against his lips. He looked at her, confused.

"I never thought I'd say this to you," Kayley told him, "but you talk too much." Withdrawing her fingers, she said, "Yes."

"Yes?" he asked uncertainly.

She laughed. He was adorable when he looked so confused. "Yes, I'll consider marrying you."

"When?" he asked, as close to speechless as he'd ever been.

"Anytime you want," she answered. "In the amusement park, if that works for you."

He laughed, envisioning that. "Lily would be thrilled."

"So would I—as long as you're the man on the other side of *I do*."

"Count on it," he told her just before he sealed their verbal agreement with an extremely long, extremely passionate kiss.

Epilogue

Maizie beamed at the young woman sitting on the other side of her desk. Kayley had all but floated into her real estate office less than a minute ago. Before she had even taken a seat, Kayley had asked if she would be willing to give her away at her wedding, adding that she and Luke were getting married.

Thrilled, Maizie had hugged her.

"This is wonderful news, Kayley, and I am absolutely overjoyed for you," Maizie said with enthusiasm. "I am also very touched and honored by your request, but I must confess, I'm also a little confused as to why you would ask me to give you away at the ceremony."

Kayley's eyes crinkled as she smiled at her. "I think you know why."

Maizie took her best guess. "It's because I told you that Lucas was looking for a physician's assistant, isn't it?"

"Well, that's partially it," Kayley replied, but it was obvious that wasn't the real reason.

Maizie thought for a moment. "And it's because I'm your godmother," she concluded.

Kayley inclined her head. "There's that, too," she allowed.

Maizie looked at her goddaughter, puzzled. "There's more?"

Instead of answering, Kayley opened her purse, took something out and placed it on Maizie's desk. She pushed it toward her godmother with the tip of her finger. "There's this."

Maizie looked at what Kayley was referring to. She raised her eyes to meet her goddaughter's. "A penny?" she asked innocently.

Kayley smiled broadly. "One of many, all of which would mysteriously turn up right in my path at the most unexpected moments." She continued watching her godmother.

"I don't think I understand," Maizie confessed. "What does this have to do with me?"

"Oh, Aunt Maizie, you are the only other person who knew my mother's penchant for believing that finding a penny was good luck. You also knew that she promised to always watch over me and that she'd drop a penny in my path to tell me that she was there, doing just that. Watching over me."

Maizie looked at her, wide eyed. "You mean you kept finding pennies on the ground?"

"On my driveway, by my car, in front of Luke's building. It seemed like every time something of importance was happening, there was a penny right in front of my feet."

"My goodness, imagine that," Maizie marveled.

Kayley laughed as she leaned forward and put her hand over Maizie's. "I love you, Aunt Maizie, but you would have never made it as an actress."

"Well, lucky for me, I don't have to," Maizie replied with a wink. "And, if the offer's still on the table, I would love to give you away."

A wave of emotion came over her. "Mother would have liked that," Kayley told her.

"Now, remember," Barbara told her granddaughter moments before the wedding march was about to begin, "don't dump all the rose petals all at once. You need to slowly scatter them all the way to the altar."

Lily raised her chin with a touch of indignation. "I know that," she answered. "I'm not a little kid, Grandma."

"Yes, I know," Barbara replied, doing her best to keep a straight face. And then she drew in her breath as she saw Kayley and her godmother come up behind the little girl. "Oh my Lord, you look beautiful," she told Kayley in a whisper, afraid that her voice would crack if she spoke any louder. Memories of how her own daughter had looked on this special day vied with what was right before her eyes now.

Barbara blinked back tears.

Lily glanced over her shoulder to see what her grandmother was looking at and smiled.

Just then, the first strains of the wedding march were heard.

"That's us!" Lily declared, and began to walk toward the altar, carefully strewing the rose petals before her as she went.

Maizie glanced over to where Theresa and Cilia were sitting toward the back of the church. Both women gave her the high sign. They'd done it again. They'd managed to successfully bring together another couple. Their record continued undefeated.

"Nervous, dear?" Maizie whispered, looking at the vision that was her goddaughter.

Kayley shook her head. "Oddly enough, no, not at all."

"I wish your mother was here to see this," Maizie told her wistfully.

"I do, too," Kayley said. At that moment, after taking a total of three steps, Lily stopped moving forward. "What's the matter, Lily?" she asked, wondering if the little girl had suddenly come down with a case of stage fright. It had been known to happen.

Stooping down, Lily picked something up and turned around to show it to the woman who was going to be her new mother. "Somebody dropped a penny right where I have to scatter the rose petals."

"Let me have it, dear," Kayley said, taking it from the girl.

"Looks like your mother's here after all," Maizie whispered to her.

"You didn't plant this?" Kayley asked.

"How could I? I was back here with you the whole time," Maizie pointed out.

"Oh." Kayley blinked back tears as they continued making their way to the altar. Maizie was right. Her mother *was* here.

Kayley kept her eyes focused on the man standing at the front of the altar, waiting for her.

Thank you, Mom. He's perfect, Kayley thought as she came to stand beside Luke.

Watching her every move, he'd seen Kayley stop and seen his daughter hand something to his bride. "Everything all right?" he whispered.

"Couldn't be more perfect," Kayley answered as they turned to face the priest.

Luke's eyes caressed her face as he said, "My thoughts exactly."

The priest began to recite the vows that would bind them to one another forever.

* * * * *

Don't miss Marie Ferrarella's next book
for Harlequin Special Edition,
THE MAVERICK'S RETURN,
the fourth book of the
MONTANA MAVERICKS:
THE GREAT FAMILY ROUNDUP
continuity, available October 2017!

And while you wait, check out some of the other
MATCHMAKING MAMAS *books:*

MEANT TO BE MINE
TWICE A HERO, ALWAYS HER MAN
DR. FORGET-ME-NOT

Katrina Bailey's life is at a crossroads, so when arrogant—but sexy—Bowie Callahan asks for her help caring for his newly discovered half brother, she accepts, never expecting it to turn into something more...

Read on for a sneak peek at SERENITY HARBOR, the next book in the HAVEN POINT series by New York Times *bestselling author RaeAnne Thayne available July 2017!*

CHAPTER ONE

"THAT'S HIM AT your six o'clock, over by the tomatoes. Brown hair, blue eyes, ripped. Don't look. Isn't
he *gorgeous*?"

Katrina Bailey barely restrained from rolling her
eyes at her best friend. "How am I supposed to know
that if you won't let me even sneak a peek at the man?"
she asked Samantha Fremont.

Sam shrugged with another sidelong look in the
man's direction. "Okay. You can look. Just make it
subtle."

Mere months ago, all vital details about her best
friend's latest crush might have been the most fascinat-
ing thing the two of them talked about all week. Right
now, she found it tough to work up much interest in
one more man in a long string of them, especially with
everything else she had spinning in her life right now.

She wanted to ignore Sam's request and continue
on with shopping for the things they needed to take to
Wynona's shower—but friends didn't blow off their
friends' obsessions. She loved Sam and had missed
hanging out with her over the last nine months. It made
her sad that their interests appeared to have diverged
so dramatically, but it wouldn't hurt her to act like she
cared about the cute newcomer to Haven Point.

Donning her best ninja spy skills—honed from

years of doing this very thing, checking out hot guys without them noticing—she pretended to reach up to grab a can of peas off the shelf. She studied the label intently, all while shifting her gaze toward the other end of the aisle.

About ten feet away, she spotted two men. Considering she knew Darwin Twitchell well—and he was close to eighty years old and cranky as a badger with gout—the other guy had to be Bowie Callahan, the new director of research and development at the Caine Tech facility in town.

Years of habit couldn't be overcome by sheer force of will. That was the only reason her stomach muscles seemed to shiver and her toes curled against the leather of her sandals. Or so she told herself, anyway.

Okay. She got it. Sam was totally right. The man was indeed great-looking: tall, lean, tanned, with sculpted features and brown hair streaked with the sort of blond highlights that didn't come from a salon but from spending time outside.

Under other circumstances, she might have wanted to do more than look. In a different life, perhaps she would have made her way to his end of the aisle, pretended to fumble with an item on the shelf, then dropped it right at his feet so they could "meet" while they both reached to pick it up.

She used to be such an idiot.

The old Katrina might not have been able to look away from such a gorgeous male specimen. But when he aimed a ferocious scowl downward, she shifted her gaze to find him frowning at a boy who looked to be about five or six, trying his best to put a box of sugary cereal into their cart and growing visibly upset when Bowie Callahan kept taking it out and putting it back on the shelf.

Katrina frowned. "You didn't say he had a kid. I thought you had a strict rule. No divorced dads."

"He doesn't have a kid!" Sam exclaimed.

"Then who's the little kid currently winding up for what looks like a world-class tantrum at his feet?"

Ignoring her own stricture about not staring, Sam whirled around. Her eyes widened with confusion. "I have no idea! I heard it straight from Eliza Caine that he's not married and doesn't have a family. He never said anything to me about a kid when I met him at a party at Snow Angel Cove or the other two times I've bumped into him around town this spring. I haven't seen him around for a few weeks. Maybe he has family visiting. Or maybe he's babysitting or something."

That was so patently ridiculous, Katrina had to bite her tongue. Really? Did Sam honestly believe the new director of research and development at Caine Tech would be offering babysitting services—in the middle of the day and on a Monday, no less?

She sincerely adored Samantha for a million different reasons, but sometimes her friend saw what she wanted to see.

This latest example of how their paths had diverged in recent months made her a little sad. Until a year ago, she and Sam had been—as her mom would say—two peas of the same pod. They shared the same taste in music, movies, clothes. They could spend hours poring over celebrity and fashion magazines, dishing about the latest gossip, shopping for bargains at thrift stores and yard sales.

And men. She didn't even want to think about how

many hours of her life she had wasted with Sam, talk-ing about whichever guy they were most interested in that day.

Samantha had been her best friend since they found each other in junior high in that mysterious way like discovered like.

She still loved her dearly. Sam was kind and gener-ous and funny, but Katrina's own priorities had shifted. After the events of the last year, Katrina was begin-ning to realize she barely resembled the somewhat shallow, flighty girl she had been before she grabbed her passport and hopped on a plane with Carter Ross.

That was a good thing, she supposed, but she felt a little pang of fear that while on the path to gaining a little maturity, she might end up losing her best friend.

"Babysitting. I suppose it's possible," she said in a noncommittal voice. If so, the guy was really lousy at it. The boy's face had reddened, and tears had started streaming down his features. By all appearances, he was approaching a meltdown, and Bowie Callahan's scowl had shifted to a look of helpless frustration.

"If you want, I can introduce you," Sam said, ap-parently oblivious to the drama.

Katrina purposely pushed their cart forward, in the opposite direction. "You know, it doesn't look like a good time. I'm sure I'll have a chance to meet him later. I'll be in Haven Point for a month. Between Wyn's wedding and Lake Haven Days, there should be plenty of time to socialize with our newest resident."

"Are you sure?" Sam asked, disappointment cloud-ing her gaze.

"Yeah. Let's just finish shopping so I have time to go home and change before the shower."

Not that her mother's house really felt like home anymore. Yet another radical change in the last nine months.

"I guess you're right," Sam said, after another surreptitious look over Katrina's shoulder. "We waited too long, anyway. Looks like he's moved to another aisle."

They found the items they needed and moved to the next aisle as well, but didn't bump into Bowie again. Maybe he had taken the boy, whoever he was, out of the store so he could cope with his meltdown in private.

They were nearly finished shopping when Sam's phone rang with the ominous tone she used to identify her mother.

She pulled the device out of her purse and glared at it. "I wish I dared to ignore her, but if I do, I'll hear about it for a week."

That was nothing, she thought. If Katrina ignored *her* mother's calls while she was in town for Wyn's wedding, Charlene would probably mount a search and rescue, which was kind of funny when she thought about it. Charlene hadn't been nearly as smothering when Kat had been living halfway around the world in primitive conditions for the last nine months. But if she dared show up late for dinner, sheer panic ensued.

"I'm at the grocery store with Kat," Samantha said, a crackly layer of irritation in her voice. "I texted you that's where I would be."

Her mother responded something Katrina couldn't hear, which made Sam roll her eyes. To others, Linda Fremont could be demanding and cranky, quick to criticize. Oddly, she had always treated Katrina with tolerance and even a measure of kindness.

"Do you absolutely need it tonight?" Samantha

asked, pausing a moment to listen to her mother's answer with obvious impatience written all over her features. "Fine. Yes. I can run over. I only wish you had mentioned this earlier, when I was just hanging around for three hours doing nothing, waiting for someone to show up at the shop. I'll grab it."

She shut off her phone and shoved it back into her little dangly Coach purse that she'd bought for a steal at the Salvation Army in Boise. "I need to stop in next door at the drugstore to pick up one of my mom's prescriptions. Sorry. I know we're in a rush."

"No problem. I'll finish the shopping and check out, then we can meet each other at your car when we're done."

"Hey, I just had a great idea," Sam exclaimed. "After the shower tonight, we should totally head up to Shelter Springs and grab a drink at the Painted Moose!"

Katrina tried not to groan. The last thing she wanted to do amid her lingering jet lag was visit the local bar scene, listening to the same songs, flirting with the same losers, trying to laugh at their same old, tired jokes.

"Let's play it by ear. We might be having so much fun at the shower that we won't want to leave. Plus it's Monday night, and I doubt there will be much going on at the PM."

She didn't have the heart to tell Sam she wasn't the same girl who loved nothing more than dancing with a bunch of half-drunk cowboys—or that she had a feeling she would never be that girl again. Priorities had a way of shifting when a person wasn't looking.

Sam stuck her bottom lip out in an exaggerated

pout. "Don't be such a party pooper! We've only got a month together, and I've missed you *so much*!"

Great. Like she needed more guilt in her life.

"Let's play it by ear. Go grab your mom's prescription, I'll check out and we'll head over to Julia's place. We can figure out our after-party plans, well, after the party."

She could tell by Sam's pout that she would have a hard time escaping a late night with her. Maybe she could talk her into just hanging out by the lakeshore and talking.

"Okay. I guess we'd better hurry if we want to have time to make our salad."

Sam hurried toward the front doors, and Katrina turned back to her list. Only the items from the vegetable aisle, then she would be done. She headed in that direction and spotted a flustered Bowie Callahan trying to keep the boy with him from eating grapes from the display.

"Stop it, Milo. I told you, you can eat as many as you want *after* we buy them."

This only seemed to make the boy more frustrated. She could see by his behavior and his repetitive mannerisms that he quite possibly had some sort of developmental issues. Autism, she would guess at a glance—though that could be a gross generalization, and she was not an expert, anyway.

Whatever the case, Callahan seemed wholly unprepared to deal with it. He hadn't taken the boy out of the store, obviously, to give him a break from the overstimulation. In fact, things seemed to have progressed from bad to worse.

Milo—cute name—reached for another grape despite the warning, and Bowie grabbed his hand and sternly looked down into his face. "I said, stop it. We'll have grapes after we pay for them."

The boy didn't like that. He wrenched his hand away and threw himself to the ground. "No! No! No!" he chanted.

"That's enough," Bowie Callahan snapped, loudly enough that other shoppers turned around to stare, which made the man flush.

She could see Milo was gearing up for a nuclear meltdown—and while she reminded herself it was none of her business, she couldn't escape a certain sense of professional obligation to step in.

She wanted to ignore it, to turn into the next aisle, finish her shopping and escape the store as quickly as she could. She could come up with a dozen excuses about why that was the best course of action. Samantha would be waiting for her. She didn't know the man or his frustrated kid. She had plenty of troubles of her own to worry about.

None of that held much weight when compared with the sight of a child, who clearly had some special needs, in great distress—and an adult who just as clearly didn't know what to do in the situation.

She felt an unexpected pang of sympathy for Bowie Callahan, probably because her mother had told her so many stories about how mortified Charlene would be when Katrina would have a seizure in a public place. All the staring, the pointing, the whispers.

The boy continued to chant "no" and began smacking his palm against his forehead in rhythm with each exclamation. A couple of older women she didn't know—tourists, probably—looked askance at the boy, and one muttered something to the other about how some children needed a swat on the behind.

She wanted to tell the old biddies to mind their own business but held her tongue, since she was about to ignore her own advice.

After another minute passed, when Bowie Callahan did nothing but gaze down at the boy with helpless frustration, Katrina knew she had to act. What other choice did she have? She pushed her cart closer. The man briefly met her gaze with a wariness that she chose to ignore. Instead, she plopped onto the ground next to the distressed boy.

In her experience with children of all ages and abilities, they reacted better to someone willing to lower to their level. She wasn't sure if he even noticed she was there, since he didn't stop chanting or smacking his palm against his head.

"Hi there." She spoke in a calm, conversational tone, as if she was chatting with one of her friends at Wynona's shower later in the evening. "What's your name?"

Milo—whose name she knew perfectly well from hearing Bowie use it—barely took a breath. "No! No! No! No!"

"Mine is Katrina," she went on. "Some people call me Kat. You know. Kitty-cat. Meow. Meow."

His voice hitched a little, and he lowered his hand but continued chanting, though he didn't sound quite as distressed. "No. No. No."

"Let me guess," she said. "Is your name Batman?"

He frowned. "No. No. No."

"Is it… Anakin Skywalker?"

She picked the name, assuming by his Star Wars T-shirt it would be familiar to him. He shook his head. "No."

"What about Harry Potter?"

This time, he looked intrigued at the question, or perhaps at her stupidity. He shook his head.

"How about Milo?"

Big blue eyes widened with shock. "No," he said, though his tone gave the word the opposite meaning.

"Milo. Hi there. I like your name. I've never met anybody named Milo. Do you know anybody else named Kat?"

He shook his head.

"Neither do I," she admitted "But I have a cat. Her name is Marshmallow, because she's all white. Do you like marshmallows? The kind you eat, I mean."

He nodded and she smiled. "I do, too. Especially in hot cocoa."

He pantomimed petting a cat and pointed at her.

"You'd like to pet her? She would like that. She lives with my mom now and loves to have anyone pay attention to her. Do you have a cat or a dog, Milo?"

The boy's forehead furrowed, and he shook his head, glaring up at the man beside him, who looked stonily down at both of them.

Apparently that was a touchy subject.

Did the boy talk? She had heard him say only "no" so far. It wasn't uncommon for children on the autism spectrum and with other developmental delays to have much better receptive language skills than expressive skill, and he obviously understood and could get his response across fairly well without words.

"I see lots of delicious things in your cart—including cherries. Those are my favorite. Yum. I must have missed those. Where did you find them?"

He pointed to another area of the produce section,

where a gorgeous display of cherries gleamed under the fluorescent lights.

She pretended she didn't see them. Though the boy's tantrum had been averted for now, she didn't think it would hurt anything if she distracted him a little longer. "Do you think you could show me?"

It was a technique she frequently employed with her students who might be struggling, whether that was socially, emotionally or academically. She found that if she enlisted their help—either to assist her or to help out another student—they could often be distracted enough that they forgot whatever had upset them.

Milo craned his neck to look up at Bowie Callahan for permission. The man looked down at both of them, a baffled look on his features, but after a moment he shrugged and reached a hand down to help her off the floor.

She didn't need assistance, but it would probably seem rude to ignore him. She placed her hand in his and found it warm and solid and much more calloused than a computer nerd should have. She tried not to pay attention to the little shock of electricity between them or the tug at her nerves.

"Thanks," she mumbled, looking quickly away as she followed the boy, who, she was happy to notice, seemed to have completely forgotten his frustration.

Don't miss SERENITY HARBOR
by RaeAnne Thayne
available wherever HQN books
and ebooks are sold!

Copyright © 2017 by RaeAnne Thayne

COMING NEXT MONTH FROM

HARLEQUIN

SPECIAL EDITION

Available July 18, 2017

#2563 MOMMY AND THE MAVERICK
Montana Mavericks: The Great Family Roundup
by Meg Maxwell

Billionaire businessman Autry Jones swore off single mothers after enduring the pain of losing both the woman he loved *and* her child when she dumped him. That is, until he meets widowed mother of three Marissa Jones, who changes his mind—and his life—in three weeks.

#2564 DO YOU TAKE THIS COWBOY?
Thunder Mountain Brotherhood • by Vicki Lewis Thompson

Recently returned to Wyoming from New Zealand, Austin Teague is determined to find a wife and settle down. But he manages to fall hard for the fiercely independent Drew Martinelli, the one woman who's dead set against getting married.

#2565 HOW TO TRAIN A COWBOY
Texas Rescue • by Caro Carson

Benjamin Graham is a former marine, not a cowboy. So when he gets a job as a ranch hand, he has a lot to learn. Luckily, Emily Davis is willing to teach him everything he needs to know. But as the attraction between them grows, Graham and Emily will both have to face their pasts and learn to embrace the future.

#2566 VEGAS WEDDING, WEAVER BRIDE
Return to the Double C • by Allison Leigh

It looks like Penny Garner and Quinn Templeton had a Vegas wedding when they wake up in bed together with rings and a marriage certificate. While they put off a divorce to determine if she's pregnant, can Quinn convince Penny to leave her old heartbreak in the past and become his Weaver bride?

#2567 THE RANCHER'S UNEXPECTED FAMILY
The Cedar River Cowboys • by Helen Lacey

Helping Cole Quartermaine reconnect with his daughter was all Ash McCune intended to do. Falling for the sexy single dad was not part of the plan. But plans, she quickly discovers, have a way of changing!

#2568 AWOL BRIDE
Camden Family Secrets • by Victoria Pade

After a car accident leaves runaway bride Maicy Clark unconscious, she's rescued by the last man on earth she ever wanted to see again: Conor Madison, her high school sweetheart, who rejected her eighteen years ago. And if that isn't bad enough, she's stranded in a log cabin with him, in the middle of a raging blizzard, with nothing to do but remember just how good they were together.

YOU CAN FIND MORE INFORMATION ON UPCOMING HARLEQUIN® TITLES, FREE EXCERPTS AND MORE AT WWW.HARLEQUIN.COM.

HSECNM0717

Get 2 Free Books,
Plus 2 Free Gifts—
just for trying the Reader Service!

♦HARLEQUIN®
SPECIAL EDITION

YES! Please send me 2 FREE Harlequin® Special Edition novels and my 2 FREE gifts (gifts are worth about $10 retail). After receiving them, if I don't wish to receive any more books, I can return the shipping statement marked "cancel." If I don't cancel, I will receive 6 brand-new novels every month and be billed just $4.99 per book in the U.S. or $5.74 per book in Canada. That's a savings of at least 12% off the cover price! It's quite a bargain! Shipping and handling is just 50¢ per book in the U.S. and 75¢ per book in Canada.* I understand that accepting the 2 free books and gifts places me under no obligation to buy anything. I can always return a shipment and cancel at any time. The free books and gifts are mine to keep no matter what I decide.

235/335 HDN GLWR

Name	(PLEASE PRINT)	

Address		Apt. #

City	State/Province	Zip/Postal Code

Signature (if under 18, a parent or guardian must sign)

Mail to the **Reader Service:**
IN U.S.A.: P.O. Box 1341, Buffalo, NY 14240-8531
IN CANADA: P.O. Box 603, Fort Erie, Ontario L2A 5X3

Want to try two free books from another line?
Call 1-800-873-8635 or visit www.ReaderService.com.

*Terms and prices subject to change without notice. Prices do not include applicable taxes. Sales tax applicable in N.Y. Canadian residents will be charged applicable taxes. Offer not valid in Quebec. This offer is limited to one order per household. Books received may not be as shown. Not valid for current subscribers to Harlequin Special Edition books. All orders subject to approval. Credit or debit balances in a customer's account(s) may be offset by any other outstanding balance owed by or to the customer. Please allow 4 to 6 weeks for delivery. Offer available while quantities last.

Your Privacy—The Reader Service is committed to protecting your privacy. Our Privacy Policy is available online at www.ReaderService.com or upon request from the Reader Service.

We make a portion of our mailing list available to reputable third parties that offer products we believe may interest you. If you prefer that we not exchange your name with third parties, or if you wish to clarify or modify your communication preferences, please visit us at www.ReaderService.com/consumerschoice or write to us at Reader Service Preference Service, P.O. Box 9062, Buffalo, NY 14240-9062. Include your complete name and address.

HSEI7R2

SPECIAL EXCERPT FROM

◆ HARLEQUIN®

SPECIAL EDITION

*Billionaire businessman Autry Jones swore off single
mothers—until he meets widowed mom of three
Marissa Jones just weeks before he's supposed to leave
for a job in Paris...*

Read on for a sneak preview of
MOMMY AND THE MAVERICK
by **Meg Maxwell**, *the second book in the*
MONTANA MAVERICKS: THE GREAT FAMILY
ROUNDUP continuity.

"Right. We shook on being friends. But…" She paused and
dropped down onto the love seat across from the fireplace.

"But things feel more than friendly between us," he finished
for her. "There was that kiss, for one. And the fact that every
time I see you I want to kiss you again."

"Ditto. See the problem?"

He smiled and sat down beside her. "Marissa, why did you
come here? To tell me that doing the competition with Abby is
a bad idea? That she's going to get too attached to me?"

"Yup."

"Except you didn't say that."

"Because I don't want to take it from her. I want her to be
excited about the competition. To not lose out on something
when she's been dealt a hard blow in life so young. But yeah, I
am worried she's going to get too attached. All three girls. But
especially Abby."

"Abby knows I'm leaving for Paris at the end of August.
That's a given. Goodbye is already in the air, Marissa. We're
not fooling anyone."

"Why do I keep fighting it, then?" she asked. "Why do I have to keep reminding myself that feeling the way I do about you is only going to—"

"Make you feel like crap when I go? I know. I've had that same talk with myself fifty times. I wasn't expecting to meet you, Marissa. Or want you so damned bad every time I see you."

It wasn't just about sex, but he wasn't putting that out there. If she kept it to sexual attraction, surface stuff, maybe he'd believe it. Then he could enjoy his time with Marissa and go in a couple weeks without much strain in his chest.

"So what do we do?" she asked. "Give in to this or be smart and stay nice and platonic?"

He reached for her hand. "I don't know."

"Your hair's still damp," she said. "I can smell your shampoo. And your soap."

He leaned closer and kissed her, his hands slipping around her shoulders, down her back, drawing her to him. He felt her stiffen for a second and then relax. "I don't want to just be friends, Marissa. I want you."

She kissed him back, her hands in his hair, and he could feel her breasts against his chest. He sucked in a breath, overwhelmed by desire, by need. "You're sure?" he asked, pulling back a bit to look at her, directly into her beautiful dark brown eyes.

"No, I'm not sure," she whispered. "I just know that I want you, too."

Don't miss
MOMMY AND THE MAVERICK by Meg Maxwell,
available August 2017 wherever
Harlequin® Special Edition books and ebooks are sold.

www.Harlequin.com

Copyright © 2017 by Harlequin Books S.A.

HSEEXP0717

EXCLUSIVE LIMITED TIME OFFER AT
www.HARLEQUIN.com

NEW YORK TIMES BESTSELLING AUTHOR

RaeAnne Thayne

SERENITY HARBOR

A HAVEN POINT NOVEL

$7.99 U.S./$9.99 CAN.

$1.⁰⁰ OFF

New York Times Bestselling Author
RaeAnne Thayne

*In the town of Haven Point,
love can be just a wish—and one
magical kiss—away...*

SERENITY HARBOR

*Available June 27, 2017.
Get your copy today!*

Receive **$1.00 OFF** the purchase price of
SERENITY HARBOR by RaeAnne Thayne
when you use the coupon code below on Harlequin.com.

SERENITY1

Offer valid from June 27, 2017, until July 31, 2017, on www.Harlequin.com.

Valid in the U.S.A. and Canada only. To redeem this offer, please add the print or
ebook version of SERENITY HARBOR by RaeAnne Thayne to your shopping cart
and then enter the coupon code at checkout.

DISCLAIMER: Offer valid on the print or ebook version of SERENITY HARBOR
by RaeAnne Thayne from June 27, 2017, at 12:01 a.m. ET until July 31, 2017,
11:59 p.m. ET at www.Harlequin.com only. The Customer will receive $1.00 OFF
the list price of SERENITY HARBOR by RaeAnne Thayne in print or ebook on
www.Harlequin.com with the **SERENITY1** coupon code. Sales tax applied where
applicable. Quantities are limited. Valid in the U.S.A. and Canada only. All orders
subject to approval.

® and ™ are trademarks owned and used by the trademark owner and/or its licensee.
© 2017 Harlequin Enterprises Limited

HQN™

www.HQNBooks.com

PHCOUPRATSE0717

Earn points from all your Harlequin book purchases from wherever you shop.

Turn your points into *FREE BOOKS* of your choice
OR
EXCLUSIVE GIFTS from your favorite authors or series.

Join for FREE today at
www.HarlequinMyRewards.com.

Harlequin My Rewards is a free program (no fees) without any commitments or obligations.

MYR17

THE WORLD IS BETTER WITH

Romance

Harlequin has everything from contemporary, passionate and heartwarming to suspenseful and inspirational stories.

Whatever your mood, we have a romance just for you!

Connect with us to find your next great read, special offers and more.

f /HarlequinBooks

🐦 @HarlequinBooks

www.HarlequinBlog.com

www.Harlequin.com/Newsletters

H HARLEQUIN®

A *Romance* FOR EVERY MOOD™

www.Harlequin.com

SERIESHALOAD2015